The Staircase of Darquata

This book is dedicated to everyone
with an active imagination; be proud
of your gift, make something of it…
It worked for me.

Mom this one's for you. Love you…

CHAPTER 1

Located on the shores of the Meskapit Sea at the harbor at the mouth of the Kabborratti River, was a small town for the traders and trappers of the region known to all as the Port of Darquata. The Port was best known for marketing fish, caught by local fishermen, who called Darquata home. Sailors knew the Port of Darquata as a comfort during the storms that overtook the peacefulness of their nautical adventures. They shared their stories of their off-shore experience catching the interests of all the people of Darquata.

Darquata was a humble, friendly town made of many little shops and stores. But the blacksmiths kept steady business going between all, making traps and repairing guns for the hunters and trappers, while at the same time supplying the fisherman with equipment. They also made and repaired equipment for the farmers of the region. Sometimes, the blacksmiths had longer days working steady. It depended on the time of year.

Darquata was recognized throughout the region for his light on the peninsula overlooking the water of the Meskipit Sea. The Lighthouse of Darquata was the highest point of the peninsula. The light of Darquata stood tall in the harbor and could be seen for miles across the waters on the Meskapit Sea.

People came to Darquata from other towns and villages all over the region. Some came from as far as Carsaria, a small village upstream on the Kabbarrotti River, while others came in on Arnagella's Trail from a neighboring town, Ippissimus. On the other side of the Kobboratti, people of Barfowler Ridge and the Mountains of Gymetaccus came for the flea markets and farmers' markets, and of course, the fish markets in Darquata. Others would come to social events, and on a clear night just to see the Lighthouse of Darquata shine brightly over the sea.

Darquata was also known for an orphanage that everyone knew as Staircase. Staircase was an old church rectory refurbished by the care and concerns of the people of Darquata. At times, many 'drifters' passing through felt it best to leave young ones, to benefit the children to a better life. Never did the children understand WHY their parents left them behind. Quite a few newborns were found along the trails that entered Darquata. Those children were introduced to Staircase with love.

Staircase was managed and operated with efforts and ideas of the town preacher, Father Gideon, and Mother Adrian, the nun of the village. Many town people contributed to Staircase giving food, clothes and even their personal time to keep the place in good, better than average, living conditions. Many people were even known to watch over the children at the orphanage, giving them things to do to occupy a child's mind, especially at the times they questioned their existence; giving Mother Adrian some well-deserved 'free time.'

As you entered the front door of Staircase, the first thing you were looking at was the staircase itself.

It was a large, beautiful staircase made of dark cherry wood that led to the second floor. So rich and majestic looking, Mother Adrian considered it the most beautiful part of the whole house —after the children, of course. In the middle of a huge dining room was a large, dark cherry wood dining room table with matching chairs. Mother Adrian managed to keep a beautiful shine with as few nicks and scratches as possible on that table set, as well as many dark, cherry wood hutches and cabinetry. The Library Room also contained bookstands and shelving made of cherry.

She tried to keep it all cleaned and polished every day. She gave everyone that same idea, developing a respect toward the fine woodwork put into the building.

Upstairs consisted of a master bedroom —Mother Adrian's, of course— and just down the long hallway, five bedrooms, a bathroom and a closet. At the end of the hallway was a narrow stairway that took you to the laundry room, the main part of the basement. On the main floor at the far side of the dining room was the big kitchen, with more cooking space than Mother ever needed. Several children could cook at the same time without interfering with each other. Mother Adrian believed that everyone should eat complete, hearty meals at the same time every day, all together. She couldn't see wasting anything, especially food! The food and other necessities around Staircase were donated and given abundantly to assist the welfare of the children of the house. Mother Adrian, in her heart, couldn't show enough appreciation to all who gave to Staircase. She only hoped the children understood how important it was to give thanks to the Lord for all that was received. "As often as possible," she told them.

Although the contributions and donations were very much appreciated, many different services were offered by the people of the village. There were always some jobs waiting to be done any time someone wanted to help improve the historic project in any way.

On one early morning, many colors of reflection from the morning sunlight shone brightly over the town off the Barfowler Cliffs. The front door of the Church of Darquata opened. Father Gideon, the town's pastor, stepped out to begin a new day. Every morning, Father started the day by ringing the church bell. But that morning, he spotted movement from the back side of the church.

"C'mon, hurry up."

It was two boys known well at the orphanage; Pete and Stanley were scampering at high speed to get back to Staircase.

"C'mon, hurry up," Stanley hollered again.

"Right, I listened to your ideas that got us into this mess," replied Peter, the other half of the team. "Actually, it's you and YOUR bright ideas that every time get me in more and more trouble. I don't know why I do this. Next time, you're on your own."

Stanley and Peter were two boys who seemed stuck together at all times, with trouble right on their tails.

Stanley was one of the kids that resided at Staircase. When Mother Adrian first took him in at the orphanage, she told him that the Lord brought him to Staircase because she "needed him there to keep her smiling." That was good enough for him.

Mother Adrian didn't realize at the time, the "job" the Lord had left for her. She always said Stanley came as a "Full Package."

Stanley was now a fifteen-year-old, curious and easily tempted. He was a boy full of ideas. He loved the outdoors. He'd rather do outdoor chores if he had the choice. If it was raining, it didn't matter to him. He'd do anything outside before he worked indoors. And, definitely, NO dishes!

Mother said, "Stanley's personality tells it all. Although he can find a great amount of trouble on his free time, he does do quite a bit of tasks for 'extra credit' which truly make up for the punishment due him, most of the time."

She added, "Then again, there have been times when Stanley can be quite a 'charmer.'" That was something Mother was proud to say.

A while back, Stanley thought of, organized, a benefit dinner, with all donations helping an older lady of the town, Martha Pepper.

"Last spring, lightning struck Martha's house. At the location of her home there wasn't enough time to save it. It was sad," stated Isabella, owner of Isabella's Kitchen, a well-run café everyone in Darquata knew of and respected.

"Stanley took on a huge amount of responsibility when he set his mind on what to do," she added. "His determination impressed quite a few people around town. Mother Adrian and I both continue to wonder just where did that kind, warmer hearted boy, go?"

Now, Peter was a totally different story. He didn't need to stay at Staircase. His parents were the owners and operators of the Traders' Rendezvous Inn, a rest spot for traders passing through time and time, again. His father, Ian, also managed the service of the Brew, a local tavern serving drinks to the trappers, fishermen, and the crews from the different ships temporarily docked in the Port of Darquata. These men knew of the Traders' Rendezvous during storms and sheltered for the winter months —even for relaxation off their ships. Captains and their crew members enjoyed the Traders' Rendezvous and all the hospitality that came with their visits.

Peter's folks, Ian and Beth, were a somewhat religious couple. Actually, Beth more than Ian, was well appreciated at Staircase. Beth was very good friends with Mother Adrian, and she knew that Mother would always keep an eye on her son any time he came to visit at Staircase, especially when it was Stanley he was there to see. If he (or more than likely, they) were getting into too much trouble, Mother Adrian usually ended up sending Peter home, and Stanley would get tasks, or chores, added to the long list of chores he had already 'earned.'

Mother Adrian and many others around Darquata knew that those two boys were quite the adventure seekers. She was glad to see the brotherhood between the two except when it was their designated time for studying, as all the children at Staircase were assigned studies each day. But she noticed that, on a good day, the two would disappear the minute they were done with their work. Sometimes they would remain gone until it was time for supper.

"I thought we'd be back by now," Peter told Stanley. "If I get in more trouble because of this so-called 'adventure,' I don't think I'll be doing much else for quite a while."

"Oh, you worry too much Pete," Stanley replied, "Just follow me and we'll be back in time, no problem at all."

Peter rolled his eyes and thought to himself, "Sure, we'll see."

Pete and Stanley made their way around the backside corner of the church, back to the orphanage with the idea that everything was clear. But as they started to dart the remaining distance back to Staircase, there stood Father Gideon with a smile.

"Hi, boys," Father said. "Where are you two headed? You seem to be in quite a rush. I hope the two of you aren't in some kind of trouble again," he said.

"I don't think we're in any trouble, Father. Uh, we went down to the river to get...."

"Now Stanley," Father interrupted. "You are aware that someone is listening from above right now. Be careful what you say before you tell it to me. For, it is He who actually does the punishment."

"Please, Father," Peter begged desperately, "I do understand your advice and I do believe the Lord is ALWAYS listening. But we do need to get back to Staircase. I understand things the Lord could do in terms of punishment, too. I only hope I can stand the punishment it's going to get us with Mother Adrian if we don't get back to the house in time, especially if my parents find out we have gotten into trouble. May we go now? Please?"

"Yes, Peter, go ahead," Father Gideon said. "I know Mother Adrian is very understanding. But just remember, she is the one who delivers the news to your folks. And Stanley, you especially should know by now what these actions can lead to."

He ended by saying, "Go ahead and good luck."

"May the Lord bless you, boys. You better hope so, anyway. WE know you'll definitely need it."

Father Gideon turned and started back into the church leaving the boys alone to think for themselves about what he had just told them.

Peter and Stanley looked at each other. Then, they took off running toward Staircase, continuing to argue about who was responsible and who was going to take the blame, although both of them knew, either way, they both were getting in trouble —equally.

CHAPTER 2

The two boys were just outside Staircase trying to decide how to get in without being seen. They went around the house and quietly entered a doorway into the stairwell that gave them the option to head either downstairs to the basement, or immediately enter the kitchen.

Peter went in first. Looking back outside, he motioned to Stanley that everything was all clear. As Stanley rushed in the door, with a confident smirk on his face, he suddenly noticed Peter wasn't smiling anymore. Little did they know, they had been under surveillance since their conversation with Father Gideon.

"I'm glad the two of you have that urge of generosity this morning. That's very unusual, I must say," said Catrina, the oldest of all who resided at Staircase.

"Oh, come on," Stanley whined. "Don't let Mother know we were out all night. We went to Talicom Bridge last night but ended up staying overnight at the park at Arnagella's Trail."

Catrina replied, "Interesting. I'm glad you like sharing your exciting expedition. Now that I have this message for Mother, I'm sure some restrictions are to follow. Who knows just what's up for you, hey, Pete?" Catrina said, knowing she had the boys to her advantage.

"Let's see, should I give her the good news now, or wait 'til you try to skip study time?"

"Give us a break, Catrina!" Stanley begged.

"PLEASE, Catrina," Peter added. "Can we be reasonable?"

"That's a very good idea, Pete. After study hour is over, the two of you can come with me to Isabella's to help her around in the kitchen, or maybe run some errands for her," Catrina said. "So don't go running off. Mother would be glad to hear your story, you know."

Catrina was the most responsible of them all. She was seventeen, but to Mother Adrian and Isabella, Catrina had started early motherhood. She was quite the help for both Mother and Isabella, making deliveries to elders around the area who in exchange always insisted she take what they offered to pay her, even though Catrina didn't believe that was necessary. If people strictly insisted, she accepted their donations and would put them toward Staircase instead.

Mother also loved Catrina's helping hand. She always loved teaching all she could to the young ones at the orphanage or other children throughout Darquata. Her kindness and maturity made most children want to be with her. It was to their advantage and, many times, to their parents, too. She read them stories or told them some of her own. Once she had their attention, they were all in their own little worlds.

Mother Adrian considered Catrina a gift from the Lord. Anytime Mother needed to count on her, whether it was running errands, doing tasks, or just watching over the House, she was there. She was a sense of relief anytime her help was needed.

That same morning, on the other side of Darquata, not far from the boatyards and harbor in the café everyone knew as Isabella's Kitchen, Isabella, the owner, sat with Mother Adrian drinking coffee and talking about recent happenings around the neighborhood.

"We could always bring the disciplinary action to beneficial advantages. They can always help around the kitchen you know," Mother Adrian said, referring to their trial and error tests of their new 'system' as she poured a cup of coffee for each.

"Oh, Mother," Isabella replied. "I thank you for all the thought you're giving toward this. But you are already sending kids to help in the kitchen now. Don't worry so much about it. You know I love those kids. They keep me smiling when they're here helping me. Especially Catrina, She's a lot of help. Besides, when she brings in the little ones from around town, they all learn more and more every time they come," Isabella told her. "And quite a few consider her their 'Aunt Catrina.'"

"Yes, but you know the question. What about Peter and Stanley? They'll probably be your most frequent workers. Staircase is known to some as a 'house of blessings.' I do think those two boys were blessed with trouble from the get-go," Mother said.

The two ladies sat laughing about what was said. Isabella then got up to run into the kitchen to check her bread baking in the ovens.

Just then, the door of the café opened and in stepped Father Gideon.

"Good morning ladies," he said. "What seems to be our subject of prayer today?" Father asked, as he joined the ladies at the table for coffee.

"Good morning Father," Mother Adrian replied.

"We were just talking about what to do with our new system," Isabella said, as she came back out to join them at the table.

"System?" he replied, as he took a seat at the social table.

"Yes. A new system we've been planning for a while, now," Mother Adrian answered. "When the kids at Staircase need to be disciplined for any reason, I'll send them here to help Isabella. Then Isabella will give them things to do to assist her around the kitchen, giving her some time to herself," Mother told him.

"Yes, Father," Isabella continued. "I will enjoy it more and more, too, especially if it helps the kids. Any extra time with the kids is 'Grandma-time."

"Actually, that sounds like a well-planned, effective system," he said. "I do see a lot of potential in this, too. As a matter of fact, I think I've found your first participants." Father said, jokingly.

"Don't tell me, Father, Peter and Stanley?" Mother Adrian guessed.

"My, you're intuitive," Father complimented.

"No, Father. They are just the most likely at this time, for some reason," Mother Adrian told him. She then got up from the table and walked into the entrance to the kitchen to put her cup in the sink. Then she turned and headed toward the main door.

"Well, I guess that's my cue. It's time for me to search for those two and catch them in the act, whatever it may be they're trying to get away with," Mother said.

"Maybe I should come with you," Father Gideon suggested. "We can discuss how things are going at Staircase."

"Father, Victor and Crendon each brought me a couple crates full of fish this morning. So, we'll be having a fish fry tonight. Mother, make sure to bring the kids," Isabella demanded. "There will be more than enough, probably plenty to take to the house after."

"I will, Isabella. I may already have a couple of servers to help you. We can test our ideas and see just what works where and how good it works. We will be here," Mother Adrian guaranteed. "Let's go now, Father. I know I'm missing something going on back at the House."

Father Gideon and Mother Adrian stepped out the door, heading down the loose stone road, leading back to Staircase.

CHAPTER 3

Back at the restaurant, Isabella started cleaning the tables. Minutes later, she walked into the kitchen and laid bread racks beside the stove. She opened up the oven to take out loaves of bread she had been baking while she enjoyed the coffee break with Mother Adrian and Father Gideon. Before she slid the loaves on the rack, she brushed melted butter on the tops, giving the whole café a very inviting aroma throughout.

Minutes later, in walked two of the local fishermen. They walked in and headed for the table just inside the front corner window. A table the people respectively considered the 'fishermen's corner.'

"Good morning," Isabella said loudly from the kitchen. "Go ahead and seat yourself. I'll be with you in just a minute."

It was the fisherman that donated the crates of fish, Victor, and his 'Ole Buddy, Crendon. They were good friends of Isabella for many, many years. The three of them grew up in Darquata. Three of the town's most well-known, most loved elders.

Victor and Crendon were well-respected in Darquata. They had a large number of children throughout the town that loved to hear their stories. Isabella would arrange a special night for all the children to listen to their interesting experiences. It really didn't matter, whether hunting or fishing expeditions, large numbers of children attended. Many parents came too, for the intense details the two men's stories brought every time they returned to Darquata and for the treats that Isabella would furnish as the children sat and listened, deeply lost in their individual worlds of wonder. That specialty made the men's stories even more inviting, each and every time the two returned.

"Oh, I should have known it's just you two.

You haven't been around for a while," Isabella smirked. "I'm having a fish dinner tonight and the two of you are to be there, too. No excuses."

Victor was a man that many of the younger generation called Grandpa. He was humorous and very loving. He always wore a white captain's hat (actually, it was gray after the many years it set on top of his head). He carried a pipe in his mouth, or if not in his mouth, in his pocket. Isabella told him he was a bad influence for the kids. He'd laugh, and then take the kids that were there at the time for ice cream. Isabella kind of admired his grandfather qualities. But she hated it when he used those qualities just to get out of 'trouble.'

The other man was Crendon —Uncle Crendon to the kids. He was a tall, brutal looking man, with the heart of a tamed bear. He, also, had high grandfather qualities. But he had one quality of his very own; any time kids were getting into, or causing trouble, all Crendon had to do is raise his voice and they'd all stopped; right in their tracks. The hardest thing about that would be Crendon trying to keep himself from smiling. Crendon was someone, the kids knew, who always had candy if they kept from getting into mischief. And almost ninety percent of the time, it worked.

Both Victor and Crendon were "salty-dogs." Each had a big fishing boat of his own, as they made their living fishing on Meskapit Bay. Seldom was there a time either came home empty handed. When they were home, they both were quite "entertaining" to Isabella. She thought they were hilarious, and most of the time, they'd prove her right.

As Father Gideon and Mother Adrian continued down the road back to Staircase, their conversation was on the system that the two women initiated.

"Do you think the fence in front of the church could use a little paint? The weather's nice lately, and it's supposed to stay this way for a while," Mother Adrian said.

"That's a great idea," Father replied. "The paint on that fence is in great need. I'm sure the people will notice the difference immediately," he stated. "I must say, Mother, you and Isabella have a way with putting things to good use; very efficient and beneficial, in a lot of ways. Thinking about it, it will be very helpful at the pig roast, too, in every part of it. From set up to clean up, it sounds wonderful. Let's just hope it works."

Father Gideon and Mother Adrian continued their way to Staircase, their conversation consisted of the conditions of the Staircase building, and the thoughts and concerns in regards to the kids in Staircase.

"Thank you, Father," Mother replied. "I want it to work, but I want it to be done right, too. I don't think Pete and Stanley will be making casseroles for Isabella any time soon. Clean-up just might be the trick there, too. But, I just know those two boys will be donating a large amount of time toward it."

"When would be a good plan to start?" Father Gideon asked.

"Truthfully, Father?" Mother asked, "I don't think there'll be too long a wait. I know those two boys are up to something as we speak; I guarantee it."

"Now, Mother," Father said, "You know as well as I, boys will be boys."

"Yes Father, but I never experienced so much trouble out of only two. There's got to be some type of explanation, don't you think?"

"Sure, but you and I both know that the Lord does his work in mysterious ways. And I'm sure those two are really going to take some time.

Father Gideon and Mother Adrian laughed as they walked down the cobblestone road, the rest of the way back to the orphanage. Once they got to Staircase, Father Gideon walked Mother Adrian to the porch and said goodbye. Then he turned around and headed toward the church.

"I will send someone to help on that fence, Father," Mother hollered. "Get everything ready. There won't be that much of a wait. Which one would you prefer?"

Father laughed. "You choose. Either one is fine by me," he said, with a smile, as he made his way back to the Church of Darquata.

CHAPTER 4

As Mother entered Staircase, she decided to make her rounds. Her first stop was to check the shoe mat at the back door. If not all the shoes were on the mats by the door, she knew who was missing in the study room.

Five, only five pair of shoes sat on the mat.

One pair of shoes was missing. Stanley was the culprit, of course. But instead of trying to chase him down, she figured she would make her rounds through the House, first. To start, she headed up the back flight of stairs to the bedrooms.

The first stop was the children's room. When she opened the door, she found the triplets, Kimberly, Kevin & Kyle, the youngest of all the residents of Staircase.

These triplets were found about two years prior. All three were discovered under a picnic table at the trail to Traders' Rendezvous, right at the far side of the Darquata Dam, at the intersection of trails up Gymetaccos Mountain.

The three kids were sweet and innocent. All were curious, and being three years old, they were willing to do everything and were quite helpful anywhere. Even Isabella would give the three different things to do. But that was only if the children wanted to.

Last, but not least, was Tara. Tara was a little older. There was only eight months between her and Stanley. To Tara, her life was, now, one big question. She continuously asked herself, 'Why am I here?"

Tara lost her mother at the age of seven. Their house had burned, along with everything in it. Her mother was fatally injured from falling rafters just before she got off the front porch on her way out of the house. This left Tara and her father alone, sad and feeling deserted.

A couple of months later, Tara's father was also found lifeless in the forest, a short distance south of Darquata.

They say he died from severe injuries when a tree he was cutting, accidentally changed direction as it fell. Unfortunately, the tree fell on him before he could escape the tree's main branches, fracturing a leg and crushing his pelvis.

Tara was on her own and living in a cave at the Ippissimus Foothills.

She was well taught by her father, very capable of surviving on her own with her loving dog, Max. Max was at her side, watching out for her and keeping her protected all the time. Some traders who spotted her crying, on their way toward Darquata told the Beth and Ian about her, and how she refused to come to town with them.

When Father Gideon and Mother Adrian got the message from Victor, they set out to find her. They found Tara and Max and talked with her for quite some time. They finally convinced her to come and join them for lunch.

Once they arrived back at Darquata, they took her to Isabella's Kitchen, where they fed her a real meal, and tried to keep the conversation going with her.

She was very shy at first, but eventually they got her to tell them what had happened, and how she came to be facing this situation. At last they got enough information to gradually introduce her to Staircase. It was a task, but they managed to get Tara to accept their help, and soon she was one more face under the wing of Mother Adrian.

Since then, Tara's been very helpful and very active around the house. She does, however, carry an attitude that not everyone can understand, making it harder and more complicated. It was a subject that Father Gideon and Mother discussed many times over, trying not to 'step on toes.' Never the less, she was soon helping out around the orphanage. Eventually, she was a pride and joy to Isabella, doing things at The Kitchen. She found things to do that she liked, but never before knew she had interest in. It was new to her, but she enjoyed it just the same.

Still, Tara was a full-blooded tom boy. Tara was a nature loving, outdoor type of girl. Mother liked that in a way. She knew Tara would be of good help for her when it came to Pete and Stanley. Tara was like a competition for the boys. Even though the two boys did a lot of trouble making, Tara could keep up with them anytime, and Mother knew it. Mother Adrian could see Tara as a big help when it came to keeping those two boys in line.

Early the next day, Catrina was about to make her rounds to the triplets' bedroom. She made a detour at the first door, Stanley's.

"Let's go!" Carina said, loudly. "We made a deal, and you're not getting away with leaving everyone wondering. There's a lot of preparation waiting to get done, but I'll be nice about it. You can do your time outside. Just remember, if this doesn't get done, Mother Adrian will be looking for you. Now, hurry up!"

"Go away!" Stanley replied, with a little whine, to sound merciful enough. But he knew too, there was no way to avoid the consequences. He sat up in bed and threw the pillow against the wall. Suddenly, he smelled bacon, and was up and dressed and headed downstairs to make sure he didn't miss out!

As Mother Adrian and Catrina, along with Stanley, entered the doors at Isabella's, many other people sat at Isabella's Kitchen, listening to the plans she had of setting up for the fish dinner. Almost immediately, Isabella began to share her arrangement for setting up and preparations, with the majority of the male participants setting up picnic tables and chairs outside on the café's patio and along the sidewalk, with enough availabilities to be safe about the size of the possible attendance.

When most of their assignments were completed, both Pete and Stanley decided to step inside the kitchen to find a tall, cool drink and take a break for a minute before they were given new tasks to accomplish. As the two stepped inside the front door, like magnets, Catrina and Isabella came walking out from inside the storage rooms, meeting the boys at the soda fountains.

"I see that most of the tables and chairs are ready. Thank you, boys, for all your help," Isabella told them. "The weather is supposed to cooperate, and almost everything is going as planned. Before we know it, this will all be history and you two will be free to go. I'm so glad you boys wanted to help." She turned away and walked back into the kitchen, ready to start preparing the side dishes she planned to serve with the fish.

"She didn't actually think we wanted to, did she?" Stanley asked sarcastically.

Stanley looked at Catrina with a somewhat dirty look on his face, and she looked him straight in the eyes with a funny smirk.

"Don't even think about it!" she told him. "Get yourselves something to drink and meet me at the backdoor. Isabella wants to scrub her back stairs to the basement, so nobody slips and falls. There are a couple of buckets under the sink downstairs and scrub brushes hanging by the cleaning supplies at the back door."

Pete looked at Catrina with vengeance. He felt tempted to beat her over the head with a scrub brush.

"I don't know what kind of thoughts are going through that empty noggin' of yours, but I'll remind you two, Mother Adrian is just an earshot away. Get it?" she said. "Go on, get started. The faster you get your assignments done, the faster I can get rid of you two." She left the two boys standing at the top of the stairs. "Hurry up, the clock is ticking," she hollered back.

Pete and Stanley scrubbed on the cement steps going to the basement, discussing their next planned adventure. Suddenly Tara stood at the doorway, just for teasing the two.

"Now I've seen everything. Well, not everything, but it's hard to believe when it involves the two of you," she said.

"Just shut your trap!" Stanley told her, aggravated.

"Yes," Peter hollered. "Get out of our sight, Tara, or I'm going to…."

He was abruptly interrupted, unexpectedly.

"No you're not."

All three heads turned, instantly, to the voice of Isabella.

"You two just finish those stairs. I have more for you to do, and I'll add more and more, every time incidents like this need attention. Tara, go find something else to do? Just stay away from those two. I could find a few jobs for you, too, you know. You can start right now if you want."

"No! Max wants me to take him for a walk," Tara replied.

Isabella disappeared from the top of the stairs. When the door to the restaurant kitchen closed, Pete took a sponge from the bucket and threatened to throw it at Tara.

"Now, get out of here, Twirp!" Pete told her.

"Yeah, get away from us," Stanley added.

"You two will never see light again. Have fun Moles!" Tara replied.

Tara went back to the top of the stairs, turned off the lights, and slammed the door, leaving Pete and Stanley in complete darkness.

"I'm going to throw her in the cow pen, just wait," Stanley said.

CHAPTER 5

Later, out by the creek with Max, Tara attempted to push over a large, dead tree trunk. The tree was big enough that it even threw mud from the bottom of the creek, splashing enough mud and water to almost cover Max. Tara could see in Max's face that he wasn't too pleased. She wrapped her arms around him and hugged him dearly.

"I'm sorry, Max," she told him. "I wouldn't have done that if I knew it was going to splash that much. I'll clean you up as soon as we get home." Once she wiped the majority of mud off him, she started her way back to Staircase.

Back in town, Tara noticed Stanley and Pete talking to someone new. She walked toward Isabella's to try to find out who the new face belonged to.

When she got in the restaurant, she hollered, "Isabella! Hello? Isabella?"

"Yes, I'm in the pantry," she replied. Seconds later, she walked out of the kitchen door to find out who was calling her name.

"Hello, Tara. How are you doing? Thanks again for taking care of the napkins and silverware. You helped save me a lot of time," she said.

"That's alright. It did keep Stanley and Pete from bothering me when they finished the jobs you gave them. Anyway, I saw those two helping a new girl down the street. Do you know who she is, or where she came from?"

"Her name is Claira. She's Martha Pepper's granddaughter. She's here from Casaria. She came to stay and help Martha through the summer, and maybe this winter. Would you like to meet her?" Isabella asked her. "I'm sure she would be glad to meet a girl who lives in the area. She may have a lot of questions about Darquata that you can tell her about. I bet she would really love Max, too. I'll bet the two of you have a lot of things in common. Maybe Claira likes to go for walks as you and Max do. But Tara, please tell me that you will not start any antagonizing between you, her, and the two boys. Martha asked Stanley if he could help Claira with preparations for the fish fry. If he can be occupied enough to keep out of trouble, then that's what it will be,"

Isabella suggested. "Please Tara, after the fish fry, you can get to know her and teach her all about your two friends."

"They're not my friends!" Tara snapped abruptly. "They're a couple of pests!

"OK, you just promise me the trouble-making can wait for now."

"I suppose," Tara replied, as she walked out the restaurant door. Even Isabella knew there was no guarantee. That's what she was worried about.

At Staircase, Mother Adrian and Catrina were doing the scheduling of the children working at the kitchen. Many of the younger mother volunteers scheduled to help with the buffet knew there would be extra time needed to organize the efforts of the little ones. Eventually, after thinking it over for quite some time, the two decided what was best and stopped their organizing dilemma. The two of them sat in the dining room of Staircase with a short time to relax. They both knew there were unknown surprises yet to come. Mother leaned back in her chair and put her feet on the stool next to her, taking advantage of the quietness throughout the house. "Do you hear that, my dear?" she asked Catrina.

"Hear what?" Catrina replied.

"That's just it, nothing. Not one sound. When was the last time you heard the house this quiet? Darling, THAT'S a true blessing!"

CHAPTER 6

The next morning, at Isabella's Kitchen, Isabella, Mother and Catrina, together, peeked out the kitchen door, only to find an overwhelming attendance of volunteers. It was a surprise to all three of them, regarding their predictions they made earlier in the week.

"I can't believe the number of people eager to take part in the servicing needed for today. I don't think we'll have trouble with keeping a clean-up crew, either," Isabella said proudly. "Unbelievable!"

"Yes, Isabella," Mother replied. "But, since the donations are for Staircase, I think we need to consider letting the kids take part in serving at the start. I'm sure they will run out of energy quick."

"In regards of the little ones," Catrina added, "I think we can let a couple of the younger mothers supervise and overlook the children seating people. At least until we really get busy. Maybe later, some could help bussing tables. Until they start breaking too many dishes," she said, with a laugh.

The three ladies then stepped out the kitchen door, into the dining room and began discussing their plan with all the volunteers to balance out the positions they had previously arranged.

Throughout the banquet, Isabella's decision to make Stanley and Peter cook at the deep-fryer, and to stay in the kitchen was a good idea. At the same time, Tara was out waiting tables, handing the orders to Isabella and going back out to get some more. The idea was working, and Isabella was proud to see the results. But, with a smirk, she also told herself, "It isn't over, yet."

Outside, Catrina watched over the little ones at the small park across the street from Isabella's, until the parents came looking for them, ready to head for home. Of course, a few of the kids wanted to spend the Night with Catrina and the triplets. With Catrina's approval the parents started for home and Catrina led the young ones back to the orphanage. She knew it wasn't going to be easy, so she started walking them around the block and through the park. She put all on the wheel-go-round until they got a little dizzy, then she put them on the grass, stumbling and laughing, enjoying the activity. She walked them to Staircase, gave them a bowl of ice cream and, not long after that, she was closing the bedroom door, where all were sound asleep.

That evening, when the buffet was over, Isabella walked out of the kitchen and sat down in the dining room. Glad to be getting off her feet. Minutes later, in walked Mother Adrian.

"Are Tara and Stanley about finished? Did they obey their instructions, without grabbing each other's throat," Mother Adrian asked, with a smile.

"The two of them, and Peter, haven't had any arguing or teasing —a true act of cooperation. Very impressive," Isabella told her.

"Very surprising; almost unbelievable," Mother replied.

Just then, out walked Peter followed by Tara. Stanley was right behind. When the three saw Mother and Isabella, they all looked at each other, wondering who was in trouble this time.

"Don't fret." Mother said. "We are impressed by your performances. See? It's not so hard to get along with each other, is it? There's no reason the three of you can't do things together—all at the same time. You proved it today. You all should be proud of yourselves."

"To be truthful," Isabella added, "This even sent me for a loop. I thought by the time we were serving, there would be chaos between you. It's good to see maturity is beginning to replace childhood. I hope it continues. Doesn't it feel good to grow up? Makes you feel a little taller too, huh?"

Pete and Stanley walked over to the table where Mother and Isabella sat. Each pulled up a chair and sat down. Tara sat on the seat along the wall, between Mother and Isabella. Then for a few long seconds; everything was silent.

Mother and Isabella, looking at each other, realized the kids were exhausted. Isabella winked to Mother, and then said, sarcastically, "OK, once we get all the chairs wiped down and the floor mats washed, you can finish and go."

All three of them looked at Isabella with surprised expressions, as if saying, "You've GOT to be kidding!"

Isabella smiled at them and said, "Don't worry, I'm only joking."

Simultaneously the three let out a large sigh and looked relieved to find out she was only joking.

"Why don't the three of you head back to the house and get off your feet," Mother suggested, "In a matter of minutes, you'll all be sound asleep. Peter, you go to Staircase, and I'll let Beth know you're spending the night. Be quiet when you get there, Catrina's babysitting and those little ones should be sleeping by now. Tell Isabella 'good-bye' and go get some sleep," Mother insisted.

The two boys said goodnight and walked out the door. Tara, unexpectedly, leaned over to give Isabella a big hug. Then she gave Mother a kiss on the cheek, told them good night, and went out the door. Seconds later, they heard, "Hey, wait up."

Isabella and Mother both dashed over and looked out the big picture window, only to see the three of them walking side by side.

"What just happened?" Isabella asked.

"I don't know," Mother answered, "Let's just enjoy it while we can."

CHAPTER 7

The next morning, Mother Adrian and Isabella sat having coffee at the restaurant, their morning ritual. Isabella began telling Mother how impressed she was and the compliments she received from others concerning the way they had organized the picnic, and how they got a lot of children taking part in it. She also gave Mother Adrian the donations from the fish fry. They both knew that it provided for the upcoming winter season at Staircase.

Isabella mentioned, "A large number of the traders gave quite a large chunk of the donation. I don't know if you noticed toward the end, many others helped with cleaning up and putting the tables and chairs away. They made the clean up fast and easy and very much appreciated."

After that week of cleaning up around the restaurant for Isabella, Pete and Stanley both thought it was time to try an adventure to get away and out of their everyday rut. They took a walk into town and ended up walking the docks. Many boats were docked, at the time, giving them new ideas for planning their upcoming event.

When they found themselves in the fisheries, they noticed Victor and Crendon, standing by the weight scales talking to one of the owners of the Shipyard warehouses, Mr. Solgood.

"I know by laws and regulations the most anyone can get per pound for ocean Salmon, is twenty-six dollars. I know that season's just about to begin and if the two of you are interested, I can keep a set price at the start. That way, we can keep track of all the fish you unload and we can keep up a steady pace for better intake and bigger production. All in all, we can all win this season," Mr. Solgood told the men. "Every time the price rises or declines, we can adjust, and I won't do anything if one of you isn't there."

"That sounds good to me," Victor replied, as he pushed back the hat on his head, scratched his forehead, and then reached for the pipe he had resting in his shirt pocket. As he began cleaning out the pipe, Crendon decided to put in his point of view.

"That sounds just fine. But I do want a copy of everything coming off my boat —on paper and signed before my boat leaves the docks. Both of you heard, by now, what that 'trusting ol' man' got out of putting the paperwork into someone else's hands. That's the worst recorded year I've EVER experienced and it's not going to happen again!" Crendon stated. "It's nothing personal. I could have made a moderate upgrade talking about the boat's physical condition. Besides, I might have to hire a couple younger boys to venture out and work for me on my ship a few times this season."

"Yeah, you are starting to look a little rickety," Victor replied sarcastically.

Out of the blue, the three men heard noise coming from behind the stack of lobster traps.

"Who's over there?" Mr. Solgood insisted. "Come out here now. You don't want to meet Ginney, my security dog. Get out here, now!" Mr. Solgood insisted, as he started walking toward the doghouse.

"OK! Hold it! It's just me and Pete," Stanley yelled. "We just came down to the docks because there was nothing to do around Staircase, and I've had enough worked out of me since that fish fry, believe me. Besides, Ginney knows both of us. She'd only lick us to death."

The three men all looked at each other and laughed. Pete and Stanley just stood there feeling humiliated about being caught in the act. Then Victor told them, "You two do a lot for my Isabella. I still don't understand why the two of you don't get something for all the work I see you doing. I'll tell you what, if you get permission from Mother Adrian and your parents, Pete, we can let you take the fishing boat, the proper poles, and all the fishing hardware out at the Harbor.

Pete and Stanley looked at each other trying to avoid expressing unexpected excitement. They never had the idea of going fishing. Better yet, this was offered by Victor. Both boys knew that meant Isabella and Mother Adrian, too, would approve of this adventure. Usually, if they approved, Beth agreed, too. Anything, as long as the two didn't blow it, somehow.

The two made an exit to the boathouses at the harbor. There they began to get Vic and Crendon's equipment for the boat down from the rafters. Both wanted to get out in the boat and go get fishing. Little did they know they were going to have an adventure that would raise the neck hairs. It would be an adventure neither of them would ever forget.

The next morning, Pete and Stanley sat at a table in Isabella's staring out the picture window into the clouds, each in their own little worlds, as they waited for Victor.

When Isabella came out of the kitchen, she noticed the two, sitting there, calmly, quietly, and immediately asked herself, "What's wrong with this picture?"

She made two milkshakes and silently made her way to their table and told them, "You two look like you just lost your favorite pets. Here you go, help me get rid of these. I must have made too many. Take them so I know you're still alive."

Pete and Stanley reacted instantly, reaching for those milkshakes.

Quickly Isabella took them away, gave a stern look and said, "I want to know what's the problem" as she returned the shakes to the table.

At that time, Victor came into the restaurant for a cup of coffee. Isabella told the boys she'd be right back and followed him to his usual table. Before he had a chance to sit down, Isabella pulled him into the kitchen door.

"Take the two out in the boat, or something," she told him, staring him right in the eye.

Victor knew at that moment he had to think of something quick. He said, "Hey you two, I'm going out in my boat. I was wondering if you want to go.

Quickly, the two finished their shakes and skipped right over to Victor's table. They started discussing the plan, asking what they should do and what to bring. Victor made a quick look to Isabella, with a smirk on his face. She smiled and walked into the kitchen.

"Good Old Grampa," she said to herself, with a pleased smile.

After talking with them awhile, Victor said, "You two better hurry down and get things put together." Pete and Stanley disappeared out the front door.

CHAPTER 8

Before daybreak the next morning, the two boys were down at the docks and waiting for Victor to show. They waited for almost an hour before Victor came walking out on the dock. Pete and Stanley, both losing patience, and trying to hurry things up, headed to the boat and began to climb in.

Then Victor told them, "I'm going to have to postpone our fishing trip. Crendon and I are supposed to take our invoices to town for tax purposes. Maybe we..."

"*#$*" Stanley said.

Then he noticed the look on Victor's face. Vic never heard words like that come from Stanley's mouth. Stanley knew right away his reaction may have killed their chance of fishing in the boat.

"HEY!" Victor responded. "I'll let that slide, but I suggest you get rid of that language. The first time Isabella hears you say that, you'll be working in the basement for a long, long time. I guarantee it."

"Sorry," Stanley replied. "We were set for this trip. I was, anyway. Back to the Dungeon, I guess."

"Wait a minute. I'll let you go out in the harbor, under one condition," Vic told them. "You don't go any farther than the Lighthouse. I'll take care of Mother and Beth, if Isabella hasn't already. Make sure you have life jackets on at all times. If I look out my binoculars and see you not wearing one, I will be out to escort you back, and that'll be your last time."

Finally, in the boat and out on the water, Pete and Stanley started preparing rigs for catching herrings and shad. Both would be bait for some bigger fish. They both learned the earlier lines are down, the bigger the fish. Now, was it a myth? Who actually cared? They were fishing!

About an hour later, the two boys finally got their heavier lines baited and in the water; one set deep and the other shallow. Four fish poles in the water and each had different bait from herring to small cod, even squid. Once they were set the boys lay on the benches, put the cushions under their heads, and started talking about the results of all the things they did at the fish fry.

"Oh, hey," Pete said to Stanley, "what's going on between you and Claire? Does she rumble your brain?"

Stanley, defensively replied, "I don't know what you're talking about. There's nothing between me and her. We're just friends. Besides, I just met her. We didn't know her before the fish fry, remember?"

Pete remarked, "Well, that doesn't matter. It's proven again and again she certainly likes you. Don't miss your opportunity. She may be your mermaid"

Suddenly, the fish pole next to Pete started singing as the line on the reel started ripping its way off the reel and into the water. As the boys realized the action, Stanley yelled, "Fish on! Grab the pole, Pete. Don't lose it."

Instantly, Pete reached out, and as he grasped the pole firmly in his hands, quickly stood and yanked as hard as he could to set the hook. Quickly he sat himself back down before he lost his balance. Once again, the reel made a whistling sound, as more line continued to go ripping into the deep, dark water.

"Wow!" Pete said, "You don't see this very often. I wonder what it is."

"Who knows, it could be a big tuna. That would be great. We never landed a tuna before. But on the other hand, it may just be a thresher shark; a worthless piece of garbage, according to Vic. Let's hope it's anything but a shark," Stan said.

"Yeah, anything else," Peter replied, holding that fish pole as if it were a fragile commodity of value, in the palm of his hands, putting the full responsibility on him. But it didn't take long for Peter to begin to tire out. After what seemed like a short stretch of time, Pete shouted to Stanley, "Here, you take over. I'm getting sore, and exhausted."

"Alright, let me get a better position. When I get started with this, I want to be ready for a long haul. That reel did some pretty sounding singing so you know that took a lot of line out. Now, let's play," Stanley said, moving into a more comfortable position, "OK Pete, gimme the pole!"

In one harmonious motion, the fish pole was in Stanley's possession. Ready for what may be a long tug of war, he began to reel in all the excess line the fish ran away with earlier. When he could feel the tension between the fish and pole, Stanley sensed that the fish had some size, too. He said to Pete, "Grab me those gloves out of my bag."

Pete picked up the bag and found the gloves. Turning to Stanley, he said, "Here, hold up one hand." He slipped a glove on Stanley's hand

and, seconds later, had the pair on. Stanley was back to fighting the fish, in full force.

For a great amount of time, the fight was back and forth between Stan and the fish. Stan would pull, reel in as much line as possible, and then, again, the fish made the reel begin singing. Stan held tension until he could reel in some more, trying to keep all the line he previously obtained. Gradually, retrieving a few feet at a time, Stanley was getting exhausted from the fight of the fish, as it got closer and closer to the boat.

Then Pete yelled out, "I see color. There it is, straight below. Keep reeling!"

"I know. Just get ready with that spear. This will be a nice fish to take home. If we get this back to the weigh station, we may get some money. But, don't plan anything, yet," Stanley said. "There it is, about forty feet, get ready with that spear."

"I'm ready. You just get it here," Pete told him.

Suddenly, right out from under the boat came a fish that was about six feet long, gliding through the water, beginning to the start of the last step of the battle. The fish drifted in a circle as it got closer to the surface.

Seconds later, the fish was on its way back toward the boat.

"Throw it, Now!" Stanley ordered.

At that second, Pete, threw the spear into the water at the fish, burying the razor-sharp spearhead into the body just behind the hard-shell gill plate of the side of its head.

"Yes!!!" Stan yelled. "Got it! Grab the tail rope. I've got the gaff. Tell me when you're ready."

Pete pulled the spear rope up, until the fish was floating right next to the boat.

Stanley, realizing no need for a gaff grabbed the tail-rope, wrapped it around the tail of the fish and pulled it, snug and tight. He gave the rope to Pete, and Pete tied it firmly on the cleat on the boat. A perfect catch, and a big one, too!

"Wow!" Pete said. "That's the biggest fish we ever caught by ourselves. What gets me is it didn't put up very much of a fight."

"Hey!" said Stanley. "That definitely wasn't easy. Besides, who landed that thing?"

"OK that's true. Still, wait till we see the faces of them back in town. Everybody's going to be surprised," Pete said.

"You got that right," Stan replied. "I think Mother's going to faint."

After enjoying a time of pride and accomplishment, they retrieved their anchor rope and began their way back to the docks in Darquata Harbor, constantly discussing an instant replay of the action of the battle, laughing and sarcastically teasing each other, until they pulled up to the dock. Stanley got onto the dock, with the tie-rope in his hand and secured it to one of the pillars next to the boat.

Before anything, Pete made sure the fish was secured to the boat. Then he reached to Stan's hand to get out. When they were both standing on the dock, they discussed the situation to decide who was going to wait there and who was running to find Victor or Crendon. They found it wasn't a hard decision. Within minutes, Stanley was walking into Isabella's front door. As expected, Victor and Crendon were both seated in the booth they considered their own.

"Hey, look whose back," Crendon remarked. "And he's not wet. Where's your side-kick?"

"Oh, leave the poor boy alone, Grumpy," Isabella said. She then asked, "Well? What'd you boys catch? Anything?"

"Did we?! C'mon, you guys have to see this fish. It's HUGE," Stanley told them. "You ain't going to believe it."

"Wait a minute," Isabella said. "I told you 'ain't' isn't a word."

"Come see this, Vic. You won't believe it," Stan told him.

"You and Crendon go with him, before he has convulsions," Isabella said. "I will have Catrina run to Staircase to tell Mother Adrian. We will be down there shortly. Don't clean it yet. Mother will probably want to take pictures."

Impatiently, and anxious to get the two fishermen to the boat, Stan gave them the story and a step by step description of the incident, and of how easily the whole thing ended. Of course, once they made their way to the dock, they began to hear the whole thing over again, Pete's version. But when all was calmed and everyone's excitement settled, Vic told the boys to start putting the poles and equipment in the boathouse and dump out the extra herring baits in the bucket. It didn't take long to get everything back to order. Then they saw Isabella, Mother Adrian, Father Gideon, and the little ones from Staircase walking out on the dock.

As soon as they could, the kids were by the edge of the dock, staring at the large, mysterious object.

Suddenly, the fish flapped its tail, splashing all the young ones and surprisingly, Mother Adrian, too. Everyone started laughing. Pete and Stanley were loving every minute of it, grinning ear to ear.

Vic and Crendon were trying not to laugh. Isabella knew what they were up to and gave them a dirty look, as if telling them, "Don't even think about it!" The two of them looked to their shoes, heads down, with grins on their faces.

A short while later Crendon had their fish hanging on the cable at the cleaning station to get its weight. Excited and over anxious, Pete and Stan found out the total size and weight of the fish.

Vic called out, "Ninety-four inches, Four-hundred and seventeen pounds. That's a good size Tuna. You boys did a pretty good job out in the boat, today. I'm impressed. You two should be proud"

Stanley and Pete looked at each other, and, simultaneously yelled, "TUNA?" and started skipping around arm in arm.

"That's a big fish," a quiet female voice complimented. "I've never seen a fish that size before."

All heads turned instantly; looking to the unfamiliar, unexpected voice. It was Claire's.

As she walked closer to the edge of the dock, Stanley said, "Be careful, that can be slippery if it's wet. Don't fall."

Mother Adrian and Isabella looked at each other smiling, trying incognito. They knew it was a serious relationship just waiting to happen. In no time at all, Isabella said, "This calls for a party, tonight, at the kitchen."

"Yeah!" all the kids yelled. After that, everyone started their way back to Isabella's Kitchen, goofing off and telling jokes, having a good old time, well deserved.

CHAPTER 9

The next day was a celebration for Stanley and Pete. Everyone was impressed by the huge fish the two of them had managed to bring in to the docks. By dinner time, the two boys had told the whopper story of that whopper-fish, as they called it, over fifty times. Of course, there were a couple of changes to the story by the time the little festival was over, but nobody even cared. Everyone agreed that they deserved the publicity and respect for the accomplishment they obtained. Both Pete and Stanley loved it, too.

As it was every year, the summer was gone, and autumn months were beginning to slow things down in the region. Although the colors and natural fragrances of autumn did make its annual entrance with the change of seasons, this year, it was more of a simultaneous conversion, very noticeable to the folks of Darquata. They were up early, every morning, aware that winter would be arriving soon and everything was needed to be prepared and ready for upcoming snowstorms. North winds that blew into Darquata, straight off of the Meskipit Sea, got quite the respect for the ice they brought in with them, year after year.

Stanley had to come in early one morning to Isabella's Kitchen to help her open the restaurant so she was ready for the customers that enjoyed breakfast there, day after day. As he walked his way there from Staircase, he noticed the quiet, frosty atmosphere and quickly picked up his pace through the cold, nippy air. By the time he made it to the restaurant, Stanley was wide awake and ready to start the day. When he walked in the back door into the kitchen, he heard a pleasant "Good Morning, Stanley. I'm glad you could come to help today. Since the ships arrived, it's been getting more hectic by the day," Isabella said.

"That's fine. And thanks for the party the other day. Pete and I really loved it. It isn't very often we get a party like that," Stanley said. "Mother Adrian said to tell you that I would be here each morning for the next week to help you open up. Catrina will be here in a little while, too."

"I'm glad to hear that. I hope you don't mind, I asked Claire if she would come in and assist in the restaurant today, too. She told me she would be in a little later, so I'm planning on her doing prep-cooking for me," Isabella told him.

"That's fine. It will be nice having someone helping out that can actually take orders without making a big fuss over what she's told to do. You know who I mean?"

"Yes, it's getting to be too obvious and expected anymore. But I will try to keep her out of the kitchen and busy in the diner," Isabella said. "Catrina is scheduled to help as a waitress, when the doors open up. Then Tara is to come in around nine o'clock. That's when Tara will start bussing tables and seating any newcomers," she added.

Stanley continued to get ready to start cooking breakfasts for the people. As Isabella opened the doors, the first people to step in were, of course, Victor and Crendon. As expected, they took their places at the corner booth where the sun was already beginning to shine in the window. Isabella immediately took two cups and their usual pot of coffee, then left them to start getting more tables ready for the crowd she knew was about to come rambling in.

A few minutes later, Claire came in the door. Isabella took her into the kitchen to give her an idea of what she wanted her to do. She needed many things prepped and cooked and ready for lunch and dinner when the time came.

Minutes later, Isabella came walking out and was pleased to see Catrina behind the counter and opening the cash register, getting things ready to handle the people and the bills they pay. It all seemed natural to her, and Isabella could see immediately she could put her trust in her if and when she needed.

About an hour later, Tara came in. She definitely showed that she wasn't too pleased to be there. As Isabella predicted, it wasn't long before she found her in the kitchen fighting with Stanley.

"Will you get out of here?" Stanley asked with a stern voice. "I don't have time to take this from you. I told Isabella I'd help her and I'm not going to let you ruin it."

"People that eat here are only getting food poisoning anyway. You can't even make a real peanut butter sandwich," Tara remarked, in an attempt to aggravate Stanley even more.

"Just get out of my face and out of the kitchen. Leave us alone!" Stanley yelled. "Will someone come and get her out of here?"

Catrina walked through the door to settle the commotion that everyone was listening to in the diner. "Tara, get out there and start doing your job. I can go back to get Mother Adrian, if you want.

Tara went charging through the door, attitude expressions making it obvious.

After a short while, Mother came walking in at Isabella's. She noticed right away that Victor and Crendon were already having their morning ritual. Now, their friends, Alvin and Marcus, whose ships were docked for the season in Darquata Harbor, joined them. They were making the morning a session of loud laughing, joking and arguing between them. Isabella told Mother Adrian it was like her 'Turkey Coop," and the men were a bunch of Tom turkeys doing their clucking and gobbling and strutting around with each other, making each morning a different session of unique entertainment. Isabella also told those men that if they got 'too loud and rowdy,' she would boot them out for the rest of the day. Of course, even though she warned them again and again, that never happened.

Still, with the noise beginning to rise, Mother gave a quick look at the guys, rolling her eyes and cracking a smile. Then she made her way into the kitchen, where Isabella waited with a hot, fresh cup of coffee.

"This is what I put up with, day after day,"

Isabella said, jokingly. "Even Catrina thinks it's funny. We get quite a kick out of some of their stories. Every day, one's story is more impressive than the rest, and then the clucking begins. It can get literally hilarious in here. But hey, if they can contain themselves, I say, 'Whatever floats the boat."

"Yes, some of it's hard to believe, but I'm certainly not going to sit here and argue; they do a good job of that themselves," Mother said. "I think that's why the women from the book club don't come around while the crews are here for the winter."

"I almost forgot, Mother, I asked Martha Pepper's grand-daughter, Claire, if she'd be interested to work for me while these guys are here. She was a real help last summer for the fish fry and I'm glad she agreed. She and Stanley do pretty good work in the kitchen, I must say" Isabella told her. "But I would like you to have a chat with Tara, right away. She wasn't here fifteen minutes and was trying to pick a fight with Stanley, again."

"I'll take care of that right now," Mother

Adrian said. She got up and walked back into the diner. When she saw Tara, she said, "Tara, follow me. We need to talk!"

Mother led Tara to the front door, out on the café patio and began by asking, "What is your problem already this morning, young lady?"

Tara began whining, "Stanley and Claire are always having fun. Even in the kitchen they enjoy what they're doing. I thought they should be working, too, like the rest of us."

"Never mind them. They share a friendship now and you are going to leave them alone! Do you hear me?"Mother replied. "Besides, it won't be long until you show an interest in a young boy. Then you won't want anyone bothering you all the time. Am I right?"

"Yuck!" Tara replied. "That'll NEVER happen! That sounds sick."

Tara went marching away, mumbling something, in an angry tone.

Mother Adrian laughed. "Just wait my little tom-boy, you're soon to be going through the same thing in a different manner," she said to herself, quietly, laughing as she walked back into Isabella's kitchen to confirm with Isabella that Tara was warned of her mischievous actions.

CHAPTER 10

"Isabella, I need some dimes for the register. Doctor Stevens is ready to leave," Catrina yelled, hoping to be heard above all the noise and commotion.

"Be right there, honey," Isabella said, as she stepped into her office to grab the needed money out of the safe.

Isabella and Mother Adrian came walking out of the kitchen. Isabella commented, "Hello, Doc.

Doctor Wendell Stevens, the doctor of Darquata. Since, well, longer than the existence of Staircase. He knew about everyone who lived in Darquata, and everyone knew him, too. Even the youngest children of Darquata admired Dr. Stevens. Maybe it was because every time they had to visit the doctor, when the visit was over, they got a sucker, or something like that. Still everyone believed the word of the doctor, they all trusted him with respect. His routines and diagnosis were very accurate and that was what the people of Darquata wanted, with no guessing involved.

"I hope they didn't irritate you enough to make you leave, Doc."Isabella then added,

"Oh, not a chance," Doctor Stevens replied. "To tell you the truth, if I didn't have to give physicals this morning, I'd be ordering more coffee. Between you and me, these boys are quite entertaining."

"Oh, you've got that right," Catrina commented.

Isabella and the doctor both looked at her, with smirks on their faces. Catrina just smiled, and then went over to start cleaning vacated tables.

That morning, everyone had the same thing on mind to chat about. They all wondered how long it would be until Old Man Winter brought in that first storm. Not only that, but just how much SNOW was going to be dumped on them to start the season?

Whatever the weather, the usual operations took place each year with ships drifting into the harbor and docked in many locations that were both convenient to the crewmen and as inconspicuous as possible. They brought the appreciated help come the cold winter season.

The deckhands loved to do their part in Darquata. Being ashore for the cold winter season didn't bother them at all. Their stay was a privilege.

The time of rest and relaxation, with the heat from the fireplaces, they waited impatiently for their upcoming departures in the spring. Fortunately, many deckhands put that energy to good use, making themselves available to anyone needing any type of assistance. Most deckhands considered Darquata a place to call 'Home.' They even felt many of the town's people as family. Most of the town's people felt the same for the crewmen.

Some of the crew members felt it was their responsibility to clear the streets and walkways of ice and snow, especially in front of the stores and storage buildings, to help keep the town's most important essentials available. Their help was the least they could do, to show their appreciation. The town's people really appreciated the ways the deckhands maintained the town's complexion, as well. Many families invited the men in for dinner and, quite often, some even gave them a place to stay, making more rooms available for the trappers and traders at the Traders' Rendevous Inn.

The heavy storms brought in large amounts of snow and, sometimes, turned Darquata into a winter wonderland for the children. Not only did the younger children look to it as a fun-time, they also looked at it as a time for them to meet new friends. Every year, there was always a couple of "newcomers" who ended up residing in Darquata indefinitely. And the tales they told of their nautical adventures always had parents exercising their imaginations, as well. The stories they told even gave the young boys ways to imagine many different snow forts and the endless number of snowball fights.

But not too many young girls wanted in on the snow wars. While the boys had their fun, they had their own seasonal enjoyment on the ice-skating rinks that the men developed on the ice at Darquata Harbor. Shoveling snow to shape the ice rinks and scraping away any bumps that may have been formed on the ice from the winds and waves whipping across the harbor, they made it a joyful activity for everyone.

Wintertime at Darquata brought in the regional trappers and traders as well. They came to unload their firs and pelts to the ships to take them overseas. Some exchanged them for new traps, or repairs on the equipment they already had. They, too, brought well-appreciated business to Darquata.

Winter made the days shorter, but in many incidents, blacksmiths had to assist each other just to find a little free time between orders. While the traders and trappers all enjoyed the company and stories of the sailors, the sailors were quite entertained by the trappers' stories and experiences, too.

Back at Isabella's, as the day was coming to a quiet, peaceful end and the daylight was fading slowly, Stanley was just finishing up with cleaning and arranging things in the kitchen for the following morning. Isabella stepped into the kitchen and saw how Stanley had developed his own routine and technique already, as if he'd been doing restaurant cooking for years. She was quite astounded and pleased to see he seemed to enjoy what he was doing.

"You can take off any time you're ready, Stanley. You've done enough already," Isabella told him. "I never knew you were such a great cook in the kitchen. It must be in your blood, hey?"

Stanley smiled, trying to hold back the blushing he knew was beginning to show. He just continued to carry on and complete all he planned to do before he left the restaurant.

Isabella then asked, "Would you like a cup of coffee before you go?"

"Oh, that's OK I want to get back to Staircase and relax for a while. That's if Tara isn't on her war path, as usual. She can find some way to irritate me, no matter what the situation," Stanley remarked. "Is she ever going to grow up?"

"Oh, come now, Stanley," Isabella replied. "If I do recall, not long ago, you were doing the same thing and acting the same way. But that was between you and Catrina. Believe me. The only difference is, the one that was doing all the complaining was Catrina. Boy, you were quite the nuisance, then, as Tara seems to be, now. That's life, just before maturity starts to kick in. Before you know it, you'll be hugging her like a little sister."

"Oh, that's just great!" Stanley sarcastically replied. "You make my future sound like so much fun."

The two laughed for awhile then Stanley put on his jacket, heading for the door.

"Thanks, again, Stanley. You're a lot of help to me, you know. Have a safe walk home and tell Mother I'll talk to her tomorrow, OK?" Isabella said.

"Sure thing," he said, as he turned the sign on the window to CLOSED. "See you in the morning."

And then, he walked out the door.

CHAPTER 11—THE NEWCOMERS

As Stanley headed down the cobblestone street toward Staircase, he started thinking of all the fun he and Claire had while working through the day. All the teasing and laughing made the day more of a game between them, and he enjoyed it. He knew that Claire was beginning to mean more to him now. Maybe Pete was right. She may have meant more to him, from the start, than he even realized. That made him start to wonder. Did Claire feel the same way toward him? More importantly, how was he going to find out? Yes, things seemed to be getting serious, now. What was he supposed to do? Who was he to talk to without any smart remarks or gossip likely to embarrass him? What was he to say to Claire?

Suddenly, Stanley's deep thoughts were loudly interrupted.

"Can I get some help?!" a voice yelled. "I need to get someone to help my brother. We were the only two left of our shipwreck, The S.S. Palatina. I don't know the cause or exactly where, but I do know we found ourselves drifted onto the beach by waves that were starting to pull us back out with the rip tide. Please, can you get me some assistance, quickly?" the man asked, carrying a man in his arms and close to breaking down from exhaustion.

"Yeah, follow me," Stanley told him, startled. "The doctor's right over here. Here, let me help."Stanley grabbed one of the men's arms and assisted, hauling him while they headed toward Dr. Wendell's office. Minutes later, he opened the office door, yelling, "Doc! Doc! We need some help here!" As he dragged the man toward the beds designated for patients in severe pain and needing immediate attention, the other unknown body collapsed into a chair just inside the door.

Dr. Wendell came into the room, quickly grabbing the injured man from Stanley, placing him on a bed. Then he dashed toward the other and assisted him to the next bed and told him to start getting himself undressed. He knew that both of them were suffering from frostbite. He asked the conscious man what they had experienced, to maybe help him give proper treatment as soon as possible.

"Stanley, go get Isabella, quickly. Tell her what's going on and tell her I need her help fast. Stop and let Heather know I need her assistance, too, as fast as possible," the doctor said. "Hurry, Stanley. As fast as possible!"

Stanley ran out the door and in a couple minutes had Heather getting ready to head to Doc's office. The minute he got to Isabella's, he started pounding on the front door. It didn't take long, and lights came on in the restaurant. When Isabella opened the door, Stanley told her what was happening, and that Doc had requested her attendance. Within minutes, the two were on their way to the Doctor's residence, wondering who these guys were and where they were really from.

Doctor Wendell was wrapping one of the men in bandages when Isabella and Stanley arrived.

Heather was washing the other with warm wash rags as she tried hard to keep the man from suffering more pain than he had already suffered. Then she treated the man with an antibacterial ointment and told him the doctor would be there to finish up.

Isabella asked the man his name, in a quiet, loving tone. "May I ask your names, and how you ended up here in Darquata?"

Hesitating, the man told her, "My name is Rahlu. Over there, that's my brother Seth. We are from the city of Dechnadi. I have no idea how far away from here that is. We were aboard the ship, Palatina, in direct course destined for Authelow, when all of a sudden our emergency horns were set off. We heard an unexpected rumble on deck and then our ship started teetering. That's when Seth and I headed for the lifeboats and assisted shipmates to get off the Palatina.

"It didn't seem like ten minutes and the ship was on her way to the bottom. I saw Captain Conway and first-mate Frasier attempt to get onto a lifeboat. After that, I don't even remember seeing them. All I remember is helping Seth onto the life raft that shipmate Skelly and I were in. The next thing I recall was waking up beached on the shoreline.

I found Seth about forty yards away and ran to get him out of the water. Once we were conscious and aware of our raft floating offshore with the tide, we realized that Skelly was farther up the shoreline. We both ran up to get him away from the water, too. That's all I can tell you now. I really don't want to talk about it anymore."

The two brothers were extremely exhausted, overcome by the strong north winds that whipped off the Meskipit waters. The both of them got severe cases of frost-bite that the doctor and Heather were in the process of treating.

Once Dr. Wendell got both of them treated in his medical room in the small-town hospital, he gave them each a small dose of a muscle relaxer to help them get some rest after their episode of seriously cold conditions. Both Seth and Rahlu were sleeping almost instantly. Dr. Wendell asked Heather to keep her eye on the two and let him know of any changes, immediately. He told her he and Isabella were going to the restaurant and that he'd be back in a little while.

CHAPTER 12

When Isabella and Dr. Wendell walked into the restaurant, there were many people sitting at tables, and some standing around, chatting about what happened to the brothers and wondering where they came from. Isabella looked at the doctor and then went to the kitchen to get some coffee brewing and bring out some cups. She knew that nobody was planning on going home soon.

When she came out of the kitchen, she knew everyone wanted to know who they were and what he'd found out. Mobbed with questions, Dr. Wendell began by trying to put everyone at ease.

"The two young men are fine. Both have some areas on their bodies that are frost-bitten, but it's nothing too severe. All they need is some rest."

"When they wake up in the morning, I don't want them to be flooded with questions, or put through any type of interrogation what-so-ever. I'm sure they will let us know of their experiences in due time when they are ready. Just remember, we have no clue what they have been through, so let's not cause some emotional or psychological stress. Let them recover at their own paces. Eventually, you will get to know all you need to know."

"Oh yes," he added, "I almost forgot. Tell your children the same thing. We don't need to scare the two brothers out of Darquata."

The following morning, Seth and Rahlu found themselves walking through the freshly fallen snow into the front door of a very unfamiliar place. Even though it was all mystery to them, there was one thing the two of them both knew quite a bit about —FOOD! And from the aromas in the air when they walked into Isabella's Kitchen, their stomachs were very much telling them, 'This is the place to be.'

Unfortunately, the minute they walked through the door they felt the eyes of the local town's people pretty obviously scanning them from head to toe. The two brothers made their way to a vacant table. Both were very nervous, not knowing what to think of the actions of the people.

"A-hum," Isabella gestured, looking toward everyone in the place with a grim look on her face. Then she walked over to the table of the newcomers, glancing around at the locals again making sure they ALL got the message. She began the conversation with a big smile.

"Good morning. What can I get you boys this morning? How about some coffee?" she offered.

"Coffee sounds great," Rahlu replied.

"That would be fine," Seth added.

"Good," Isabella said. "I'll be right back."

As Isabella turned her back to the boys, she again gave that look to everyone.

Soon, she returned to their table, Isabella said, "Here you go. Two freshly brewed morning coffees. Believe me, if anyone says 'NO' to MY coffee around here, they must be coming down with something." Isabella said jokingly.

The two of them looked at each other, then back at her, with puzzled looks on their faces, both cracking a smile to her sarcasm.

"Now, what can I get you two for breakfast this morning?" Isabella asked.

"Oh, the coffee's good enough," Seth told her.

"Oh, c'mon now, you boys look like it's been quite awhile since you've had a real, home-cooked meal. And don't worry about it—it's on the house, I insist! This is Isabella's Kitchen, and I'm Isabella. What I say goes," Isabella said, with a big smile on her face.

This time, Rahlu got the joking part of it all and gave a little chuckle. But Seth, again, hesitated. Only seconds later, he cracked a smile, too.

Then he said, "Thank you. We really appreciate it. We'll be glad to work it off."

"Don't even think about it!" Isabella interrupted. "It's on the House. Don't you remember what I said? 'This is Isabella's Kitchen. I'm Isabella. What I say goes!'" She said with a big smile on her face, as she handed them each a menu.

"OK, thank you," Seth said, quietly.

"Yes, thanks," Rahlu added.

"Now, that's what I like to hear. I'll be back when you are ready, to take your orders," Isabella said. She turned and headed toward the kitchen.

As she walked away, Seth and Rahlu both glanced around the dining room noticing everyone looking their way. Only now, the people all had a neighbor-like smile on their faces, even though a few still looked a little mystified.

Over at Staircase, Mother Adrian had just made her rounds, as usual, to get the kids up, out of bed, and downstairs for breakfast. When all was accomplished, Mother headed back down the stairs. As she stepped into the foyer on her way to the kitchen, she almost ran into Catrina who was headed to the kitchen as well.

"Mother, Stanley told me last night, that a couple of guys wandered into town. He said they were in pretty bad shape and Dr. Wendell took care of them. Have you heard anything about it?" Catrina asked.

"No, I haven't heard anything about that. I didn't even hear Stanley walk in last night. I'll have to talk to Doc or Isabella to get the details. Did Stanley get up to go to work on time?"

"I guess so," Catrina answered. "He was already gone when I came down this morning."

"Wow, that boy's beginning to amaze me—if that's where he is?" Mother said, with a small sense of doubt fluttering in that statement. "What time are you to be there this morning, Dear? Mother Adrian asked.

"Isabella told me any time after the kids are off to school would be fine. I'm hoping to be there before 10:00," Catrina replied.

"They always need to be tamed, you know," Mother told her, with a smile.

Catrina laughed and went into the kitchen to finish making breakfast for the kids. Minutes later, she headed upstairs to get ready to work, all the while anticipating what there was yet to learn about the new-comers.

Back at Isabella's, as the two brothers were finishing up with breakfast, a sudden shadow darkened their table. Seth and Rahlu turned to see the cause of the darkness, with defense in mind.

CHAPTER 13

"Let me introduce myself," the huge body suggested. "My name is Crendon. I'm one of the locals from around this fish town. You see that table over there?" he added, as he pointed his finger toward the designated table in the corner. "We all want to invite you over to join us, and hopefully, make you more comfortable while you experience the outcome of your trauma. If you need any assistance, feel free to ask anybody. We're here to help."

"Thanks, but I'd rather not just yet. My brother and I need to do a little more recuperating. This is a real change for us. It's nothing personal, you know. Do appreciate the offer. How 'bout we get back with y'all on that a little later?" Rahlu asked.

"No problem. I understand, but anytime you two need someone to talk to, just c'mon over and join us," Crendon said.

"OK, we'll do that. And thanks again," Seth replied.

Crendon walked back to the 'turkey table' and let the crowd know they were not quite ready to open up. So, the decision was made to let them relax.

Just a few minutes after, Mother Adrian and Father Gideon walked into the diner, to the counter.

"Hi Isabella. Mother and I will take our usual," Father Gideon said.

"OK," she replied. "Let me deliver this order and I'll bring your coffee."

"Bella, we'd like to talk to you whenever you've got a minute," Mother said.

When Isabella walked out the kitchen door with the coffee for Father and Mother Adrian, the three of them started chatting in a low tone of voice, until Isabella went back to the kitchen.

Mother Adrian and Father Gideon walked over to Seth and Rahlu and introduced themselves, expressing a friendly kindness to the two men.

"Good morning. My name's Father Anthony Gideon, everyone just calls me Father Gideon. This is Mother Adrian Rominette, or Mother Adrian," Father told them. "We'd like to offer you a comfortable place to stay while you are with us in Darquata. Mother manages a place down the road called Staircase. Staircase is actually an orphanage for young children found in the area who are deserted by their parents for some reason or another. At the moment, we have extra room at Staircase and would like to offer you a place to stay. At least until the two of you decide what it is you want or need to do. What do you say?"

Seth and Rahlu looked at each other for a moment. Then Rahlu said, "We'd really appreciate it. Actually, in a way, that's what we were talking about. We heard a couple people down the street talking about it as we walked by. I was beginning to wonder myself."

"Great. Then we'll take you to Staircase when you're finished. But you two take your time, there's no hurry."

Mother Adrian and Father Gideon stepped back to the counter to have their coffee and discuss all that had to be prepared for the new residents at the home. They both knew the two men were ready to get some serious rest and much more sleep than they had since they arrived.

When the two men were finished, the four of them left Isabella's, heading for their new place to reside, chatting and discussing things with the idea of getting to know more about each other and more about Darquata. They walked at a steady pace to overcome the cold of the winter.

Their arrival at Staircase was a true welcome, with the triplets running to meet them inside the front door. Seth was startled at first, but within minutes he was almost as entertained as the kids. The three little ones began asking crazy questions, though none that a young child wouldn't want answered.

"Where are you from? Is he really your brother?

Do you know how to make a snowman?"

That's when Mother Adrian told them, "Kevin, Kyle and Kimberly leave the two alone. They just got here. Why don't you three go get ready for school? It's getting late. Kyle, you make sure you put your pajamas in the hamper, or I'll make you wear the same dirty pair tonight. Now, you three get going."

All three said "Goodbye" to Seth and Rahlu, and then unexpectedly, all three walked over to give them each a hug. They turned and dashed toward the big staircase and raced up to the top.

"Settle down, you three!" Mother Adrian yelled. "If I have to come up there, you're all going to get a spanking!"

At that moment, Seth looked Mother in the eye, perplexed, never thinking that something like that would come out of Mother's mouth.

Mother Adrian smiled. "I could never do something like that to those three. Actually, compared to a couple other residents that joined us here at Staircase, those three are my 'Angels.'

"Oh, that's good to hear. I've never seen a nun spank a child before," Seth replied. Rahlu just chuckled. He knew that would never happen. Then he turned and gave his brother a little punch in the arm.

Mother also expressed a small laugh and said, "Why don't you two follow me? We have to go up there to show you the room I have ready for you. Besides, ten to one, I'll have to be up there shortly, before one of the boys starts beating on the other. Kimberly's nothing to worry about. She sleeps in a different room with Catrina. She's quiet as a mouse most of the time."

Mother walked to the big staircase and started up the steps with Seth and Rahlu right behind. Rahlu was fascinated by the size of the staircase and by the whole size and design of the place. He was truly impressed with the dark, hardwood stairs, cabinets and trim throughout the whole house. To him, a place like this, with an opulent structure and design, would only belong to a wealthy, respected, hierarchy back home. It took him a while to let it sink in that the Staircase was, surprisingly enough, an orphanage.

Upstairs, as Mother led them down the hallway, she pointed out which rooms were bathrooms and then described what bedroom belonged to whom. As she headed toward their designated room she stopped and said, "If you need anything, or have any questions, feel free to ask Stanley. That's his room right over there," she told them, pointing across the hall. He should be coming home anytime, now. He knows anything you'd like or need to know. Truthfully, I think Stanley knows more than I do. Sometimes I wonder if he's got some secret trap doors. He sure gets out of the place, if he's determined, no matter what the situation may be. Now, you two go ahead and get yourselves situated and, like I said, Stanley will be here shortly if you need anything."

"Thank you, again," Rahlu told her.

"Yes, thank you," Seth added.

"Oh, it's no problem. I'm glad we have the room. Besides, I talked to Beth, out at the Traders' Rendezvous, the inn at the edge of town and she said that she and Ian, her husband, have an extra room for you there soon. It's quiet and you don't have kids asking questions constantly. Father and I think you two will like it. Beth is eager to have you. Now, go ahead and make yourselves at home. Feel free to sleep in as long as you want in the morning. I'll try to keep the kids from pounding on your door. Catrina's up early to take care of them, anyway. I'll see you in the morning." Mother said, as she exited the room, closing the door behind her.

"Wow! This place is better than the Portage Hotel back home," Seth commented as he got himself undressed and jumped into one of the beds. "And, I must say, this bed is nice!"

"Yeah, just get some sleep. We don't know what tomorrow's going to be like. You heard her. We don't need to get up right away. I, myself, am going to obey her rules. Now, go to sleep," Rahlu insisted.

Seth got up, stepped over to shut off the lamp by the window and found his way back to his bed. When he was all tucked in and relaxed, he sighed,

"Ahh." Then he rolled over and faded away in no time at all.

CHAPTER 14

The next day, when Rahlu woke up he noticed his little brother was already up and gone, but that wasn't really important to him at the time. He just rolled over and started to drift back to sleep. He wasn't going to let a privilege like this one slip away. Besides, his little brother should be able to manage, he thought, with closed eyes and a smile.

Downstairs, Seth was in the kitchen, already answering questions the kids were throwing at him. He loved it. Never before had he entertained kids so much. To think, he wasn't doing anything at all but telling them his life story, in a way.

"Where did you come from?" Kimberly asked.

"We are from Dechnadi," Seth told her.

"What's Dek-nah...? Kyle asked, trying to pronounce it himself.

"Dechnadi. It's a small town far away from Darquata. We really didn't plan to come this far from home, but the boat we were on sank to the bottom and we had to swim to shore," he said. "Now, why don't you tell me about you, like what are your names and how old are you?"Kimberly's hand shot right up in the air and she immediately began telling Seth, "My name's Kimberly, I'm five. This is my brother Kyle. He's five, too. Our other brother is Kevin. He's also five."

"Oh, so you are triplets? Seth asked, jokingly. "I only have one brother. His name is Rahlu. He's the one sleeping upstairs. He's older than I am. But that doesn't make a difference. We do almost everything together. How long have you been here at Staircase?"

That's when Catrina came walking into the kitchen.

"Are you three bothering this man already?

Why don't you all go up and get dressed? I'll be right there shortly. Last one up is going to help clean the kitchen, so you better get going."

The three headed out of the kitchen, through the dining room, and started racing each other up the stairway, pushing and shoving to be first one to the top, hollering and whining to each other for unnecessary reason, all the way to the top.

"If you don't quit arguing, all three of you are going to clean the laundry room, too!" Catrina yelled back, with a smile on her face. "It never works, but they do quiet down. Hi I'm Catrina. I stay here at Staircase. I help Mother Adrian take care of everyone, the kids I mean, to do their chores around the house. Truthfully, I also work over at Isabella's this time of year. Sorry to be rude, but you saw what I have to take care of before they start beating on each other. I'll probably see you over at the restaurant a little later." Catrina headed to the stairway and started raising her voice to the kids before she got to the top.

That afternoon, Rahlu and Seth decided to head back to Isabella's and hopefully, find out more about Darquata, and maybe find out just how far they were away from their home, Dechnadi.

When they arrived, they noticed only a couple of the morning bunch were at the corner table. They walked over to the same table they had before and sat down. Minutes later, Catrina was there to take their orders.

"Hello, I'm Catrina," she told them with some sarcasm, since she had already introduced herself to Seth that morning. Then she said, "I will be your waitress today. Actually, I'm the only waitress so you don't have much of a choice."

Both men started laughing. Then Seth added, "Well, it's nice to meet you. I'm Seth and this is my brother, Rahlu. He's the older one. Actually, he's already over the hill"

Suddenly, THUMP! Under the table Rahlu kicked Seth for making that smart remark. All three of them laughed.

"Oh, that's nothing like those old 'geezers' from the 'turkey coop'" Catrina said.

"Turkey Coop?" the two asked.

"Yeah" Catrina replied, adding "that's the big table over there in the corner, by the window. Usually, it's Victor and Crendon, and Mr. Solgood. Victor's the old man with white hair and the pipe in his pocket, if he's not smoking that nasty thing. Crendon's the big one. But don't worry about him. He may look big and mean, but, believe me, he's just a teddy-bear."

"The third one of the bunch is Mr. Solgood. He owns the fisheries across the harbor. He's more of a quiet type. But when the crew comes in and starts laughing and hooting and hollering, he can get very loud and noticeable," Catrina ended

"Wow, it sounds like those guys are the life of the place," Rahlu replied.

"Not really," Catrina answered back. "After you get acquainted, they can be more of a nuisance than anything. Believe me, I know from experience. The rest of the guys are only here for the winter months. Oh, you don't know how I look forward to spring!"

"Isabella's must be a busy place throughout winter," Seth said.

"Not really, most of them order the same thing over and over, if they order anything at all. I think their main staple is coffee. When all those 'hoots' are here, all I'm doing is making coffee, in between running other people their orders," Catrina told them.

"Awe, that sure doesn't sound fun," Seth said.

"Boring is the word. But Isabella deserves the help after all she does around here."

"Catrina, orders up!" yelled the voice from behind the kitchen door.

"You guys decide what you want to eat, and I'll be back shortly. Maybe you two can tell me about yourselves," Catrina said as she headed to the kitchen door.

In the kitchen of the restaurant, Stanley was waiting for Catrina to come and get the food plates out of the window so he could continue putting out his orders.

"C'mon Catrina, it's not really time to socialize, right now. Besides, I don't think your 'prince charming' is going to be leaving anytime soon. I don't think others like their plates cold. Breakfast is the most important meal of the day. Frozen isn't acceptable," Stanley told her, with a touch of sarcasm.

"Oh, stuff it!" Catrina replied. "I never bothered you when you were all warm and cozy with Claire. I want to help Seth get the horrible parts of their experience off his mind. I'm not getting warm and cozy. I'm just interested."

"Fine, just take these plates out so I can keep up with the orders," Stanley demanded.

"Fine," Catrina said. "Give me a minute while I seat those newcomers. I'll be right back."

"Hurry up," Stanley ordered as she disappeared out the door to the dining room. "I don't know how she keeps that job" he said to himself.

A few days later, on another sunny wintery morning, Stanley was at Isabella's doing, what seemed to him, as suffering a long, hot, scorching morning; just one more morning of ovens, stoves and hot grills and boiling kettles in the kitchen.

As he finished preparing meals for that day's dinner service, he was suddenly interrupted by Isabella as she walked into the kitchen.

"Stanley, I can handle the kitchen for the rest of the morning," Isabella told him. "The dining room is pretty dead this morning. There's only Beth and Mother Adrian and me having coffee out there. Mother said that she feels you earned the day off."

Scratching his head, with sarcasm he replied, "Really? Who put sugar in her coffee cup?"

Isabella laughed and shook her head as she went back out to join the other ladies.

As the kitchen door swung closed behind Isabella, Stanley yelled, "Don't tell her I said that!"

Stanley finished prepping what he was doing for lunch, grabbed his jacket and hat, and sprinted out into the dining room, heading for the restaurant's front door.

"Hold it, Mister," Mother insisted. "You know there's a catch, right? Come over here and sit down for a moment. We have to talk."

Instantly, that excitement and adrenalin seemed to have died in him. He turned and pulled up a chair and sat down at their table.

"Beth has a favor to ask you," Mother said.

Stanley looked a little puzzled and confused.

"I wondered if I could ask you to help Peter for the rest of the day. I know he couldn't do it alone, and I figured the two of you wouldn't have any trouble getting it done," Beth told him.

"Sure. What's the job?" Stanley asked, in a somewhat depressed manner.

"I was wondering if you'd take him ice fishing?" Beth asked him, trying to sound serious, without cracking a smile. But that didn't work.

Stanley's thoughts immediately caught attention to what Beth just said. His eyes opened wide, his head popped up and his back straightened to complete attention. Unexpectedly enough, he almost fell off his chair.

Isabella, Mother Adrian and Beth couldn't keep from cracking smiles at Stanley's reactions. All three of them were fighting hard not to laugh.

"You're kidding, right?" Stanley asked, and then added, "Jokes like that aren't funny to me. Seriously, what was the favor?"

Beth told him, "No joke. Pete and his father were supposed to go ice fishing last weekend, but he's been so busy with the Inn he can't keep up with the time. I figure if Pete can have someone go with him, I'll be glad to let him go. Ian would love you for it, too. But, there's one condition…."

"Sure, what's that?" Stanley relied, all hyped up with excitement and anxiety.

"The two of you go to Ian's shanty out on the harbor, nowhere else. Do you hear me?" Beth said.

"No problem. When is Pete going to be ready?"

"Oh, he's ready and waiting. Go get your stuff ready and I'll have him meet you at Staircase. And make sure you dress warm!" Beth said to him.

"That's fine!" Stanley remarked. With no hesitation, he was out the restaurant door, pushing a new, direct trail through the fresh fallen snow straight back to Staircase.

"I told you he'd go," Mother Adrian said with a laugh.

Then suddenly, Isabella got a safety harness on the whole plan. She told Beth and Mother, "Hey, why don't we see if those two new guys may want to go, too…to keep an eye on them."

Mother and Beth looked at Isabella, then at each other and back to Isabella.

"What are you thinking?" they said, looking at Isabella and the mischievous smile she had on her face.

Together, the three women crowded around the table quietly discussing her new part in the boys' upcoming fishing expedition.

Minutes later, Beth got up, took her coffee cup to the kitchen, said good-bye, and walked out the door. She was impressed by how Isabella came up with her idea. It didn't take long for her to get to the inn and get in touch with Seth and Rahlu.

CHAPTER 15

When the two brothers met Beth in her kitchen she asked, "I was wondering if you boys would like to do me and Ian a favor. Pete, our son, has been asking Ian to take him out to their shanty to go ice fishing. I already told Stanley that I was going to let them go out but, I still feel those two could use a little parent-type company. Just to make me feel better. Are you interested?"

The brothers looked at each other.

"No problem. I'm game," Rahlu responded. Seth didn't reply. The look on his face didn't seem interested at all. He seemed to have something else on his mind and was deep in thought at that very moment.

Beth said to them, "Even if it's just one of you, I will still feel a lot more comfortable knowing someone is out there with those two."

That afternoon, while Pete, Stanley and Rahlu were out in the shanty, Seth went back to Isabella's to find out when Catrina would be getting out of work. He knew it was easy to talk about things with her, even easier than it was with his brother. When he opened the door, all heads turned to look at him as they did ever other time he entered. But this time, he seemed to have gotten used to it and nodded his head to everyone staring. That made it clear that he was just as much a regular customer as them now.

When he sat down at the table, Isabella was first to say something.

"Hello, Seth, how's the day going for you? I see you didn't prefer to go fishing with the rest of the boys. Is there something wrong? Are you not feeling alright, today?" Isabella asked.

"No, I'm fine. I like fishing, but I don't prefer the cold part of it just yet. It's a lot nicer in here." He replied.

"I agree with you there," Isabella said. "I'd rather be wrapped up in my afghan and reading at home, myself. Do you want coffee?"

Seth said, "Sure, thanks Isabella. Do you know if Catrina's still here?"

"Yes, she's in the basement right now," Isabella replied. "How 'bout I have her bring you your coffee? She's done working for today. Would you want something to eat?"

"No thanks, the coffee's just fine," Seth told her.

Isabella went to the kitchen and to the stairwell to the basement, saying, "Catrina? Can you come up here for a minute?"

As Isabella waited up in the kitchen, she heard footsteps coming up the stairs, getting closer and closer, until Catrina came out from the doorway and said, "Do you need something, Isabella?"

"No, I don't need anything. But someone requested your service. He wants coffee," Isabella told her, with a huge, smiley expression on her face.

Catrina looked at her, puzzled, wondering what that look was for. She grabbed a pot of coffee and a cup and went out to service this 'someone.' When she realized that special someone was Seth, she looked back at the kitchen door only to notice Isabella peeking out the small glass window. As she realized the trick Isabella had played on her, she looked at her and shook her head, with an unpreventable smile as she took Seth a pot of coffee.

"Oh, you're back?" Catrina asked. Little did Seth know Catrina was really pleased he didn't go with the others out to the shanty for the day.

"I didn't want to go out on ice and freeze just yet," Seth told her, jokingly. "I'm feeling fine right here, without frostbite, and without my brother, just the same."

They both got a chuckle out of his reply. Then he added, "I was wondering, what time do you get done working today. I thought I'd walk with you back to Staircase if you want?"

Catrina replied, "I'd like that. I'm scheduled to work until five o'clock. But if you want to wait, we can get something to eat before we leave. Mother Adrian will feed the little ones and everything in the kitchen will be done. First, let me take care of these folks at the other tables and then I'll ask Isabella."

"That's great," Seth said. "I'm in no hurry anyway. I'll wait right here."

Catrina was heading toward the other tables when she realized she still had the coffee pot for Seth in her hand. She turned around to run it back.

"I'm so sorry," she apologized, embarrassed, as she poured him a cup of coffee. She put the pot on the table blushing deeply.

"It's no big deal. I'm not one of the important customers. Go take care of them. I'll wait right here," he told her.

Catrina made her rounds, taking orders and removing dishes from people already done eating. She turned and headed to the kitchen to put in new orders. She walked into the kitchen and found Isabella standing behind the grill, waiting impatiently for her. She noticed that Isabella was eager to find out the results of her instigative devilry.

"Well? What did he have to say?" Isabella asked impetuously.

"Why did you do that? That made me embarrassed," was the reply.

"See? The two of you do have interests. As it seems, the two of you enjoy being together. So, why don't you go out there and keep him company? Don't worry about me in the kitchen. I've done this for years. Besides, there are not enough people out there to keep me busy. So, take off that apron, put your pleasant smile on your face, go out there and enjoy yourself with the young man. Go. Now, get out of my kitchen! Have some fun," Isabella said empathetically.

Catrina took off her apron, brushed off her blouse and stepped in front of the office door in the kitchen, looking into the mirror to straighten her hair and examine her appearance.

"Go! I don't think he cares what your hair looks like. He's waiting for you. Go, have fun," Isabella told her tauntingly.

When she was halfway across the dining room, Seth noticed her without her apron. He instantly stood up and politely assisted her to the table.

Watching from the kitchen door window, Isabella couldn't keep a tear from running down her cheek. She was so glad she could do something like this for Catrina. She also knew Mother Adrian would think the same and when she found out, Mother, and Beth, were both going to smile from ear to ear.

"Boy, that was quick," Seth said.

Catrina instantly replied, "She had all of this planned, I know it. When I went into the kitchen it seemed she was ready to send me right back."

CHAPTER 16

Out in the shanty, the three excited fishermen were just getting things set up. While Rahlu started a small fire in the shanty's little wood stove, Pete made four holes in the ice, for the four corners of their larger sized fishing hole for them to fish through and for the bait bucket. At the same time, Stanley took his auger and a bucket full of tip-ups and headed out a distance from the shanty and set tip-ups. He drilled six individual holes in the ice, two for each of them.

He went back to the first hole, drilled, and started putting a tip-up line, properly baited with a feisty minnow which was a reasonable size weight to keep the minnow at the specific depth chosen to fish. Then he took the trip flag, which was the part of the tip-up and placed it not only to hold the steady depth of the bait, but also, when it was 'tripped' by a biting fish to let the fisherman know there might be a fish on that line. It was a time-consuming job, but to him, it was worth it.

Once the first tip-up was set, Stanley continued the same technique for the remaining five, each one set at a different depth. Eventually, he had completed an ice fisherman's major task of setting up and headed back to the shanty.

When Stanley got back to the shanty, he knocked to get one of the others to unlock and open the door. "C'mon, open the door," he hollered. "My hands are frozen stiff."

A small noise of the latch on the door snapped and slowly the door opened. Stanley grabbed the outer handle on the door and quickly stepped his way into the shanty, closing the door behind him.

For a few seconds, Stanley's eyes had to adjust to the brighter light of the lanterns; one on the floor next to Peter's fishing pole and the other hanging from the ceiling in the middle of the interior.

Now, they knew everything was set.

"Let the fishing begin!!" Rahlu said, with a little extra gung-ho voice.

For a while, Pete and Stanley told Rahlu of many things the two of them did; good and bad, and emphasizing the 'Lucky' ones. Eventually, the three of them were all laughing loud and jolly with Pete and Stanley trying to keep each other from losing their balance and possibly ending up down the hole.

"Pete! Your pole!"Rahlu yelled.

Instantly, the two boys quit the horsing around and converted to serious fishing. Pete's eye and attention were pinpointed at his fish pole, staring at the tip of the pole, intensely waiting for that fish to bite again.

Rahlu and Stanley sat back on the bench to relax a bit and stay out of Peter's way. As Stanley turned to grab his thermos full of coffee, he noticed Rahlu making a gesture to him behind Peter's back.

By hand gesture alone, Rahlu made the moves to tell Stanley, 'That's not real, watch this!'

Patiently, Stanley kept his eye on Rahlu, waiting to see what he was secretly planning for Pete. A couple minutes later, Peter put down his pole, turned toward Stanley and shrugged his shoulders. That's when Rahlu made his move.

Previously, when he and the two boys were laughing and horsing around, Rahlu had reached down and picked up a couple pieces of ice and had them setting on the bench between his legs. That's where all of it started, the chaos of Pete's notorious fish bite.

As Pete started to say something to Stanley, Stanley sat with his eye unnoticeably on Rahlu. Rahlu tossed a small chunk of ice at the tip of Peter's pole, making a small splash in the water just in front of it. This time the deceiving actions caught Pete's attention.

Peter was sitting awkwardly on his chair. In his outright attempt to grab his fish pole, he lost his balance, falling straight toward the fishing hole on his way to an extremely frigid outcome. By pure luck alone, Stanley reached out and grabbed the back of Peter's jacket and pulled him away from the hole with all the energy he could muster, sitting him back on his chair.

Peter, retaining his balance, accidentally kicked his lantern and the three of them watched it slowly sink to the bottom of the harbor. Due to the fact that the lantern burned oil, the light of the lantern shined for extra seconds while it sank in the water, gradually getting darker, until suddenly, everything was dark beneath them.

After the unexpected event was over, Stanley looked at Rahlu somewhat horrified. Rahlu looked back at Stanley just as puzzled. The two of them looked toward Pete.

There sat Peter, staring motionlessly down the big fishing hole, confused about what had just happened.

A few minutes later, Rahlu picked up his pole and started re-rigging his line

"Stanley, do you have a couple treble hooks," Rahlu asked, sort of hushed about it.

Stanley pulled his fishing bucket to his feet and got out his compact tackle box. After looking in it for a few seconds, Stanley came up with all of his existing treble hooks and presented them to Rahlu, wondering what his new friend was about to attempt.

When Rahlu picked out the biggest treble hook Stanley had available, he tied three of them onto his line and put a heavy weight at the end of the whole set-up. Then he dropped the line to the bottom. After his line became slack, he reeled up enough to make it taut and started jigging the pole with somewhat long retrieves, up and down continuously.

This went on for a few, somewhat long minutes, until suddenly Rahlu said, "Hey guys, I've got something!" His fish pole bent almost to the floor of the shanty.

As Pete and Stanley watched Rahlu fight the mysterious type of fish, their eyes were tightly focused on the hole. Rahlu then said, "Stanley, grab the gaff hook."

Stanley noticed Rahlu shaking his head unseen to Peter, and Stanley knew that whatever was on the end of that pole was not a fish.

Peter, on the other hand, still sat with his back hunched over and his eyes seriously focused on Rahlu's upcoming catch.

Again, Rahlu caught Stanley's attention, silently signaling to be ready for the next episode of their fishing adventure. Seconds later, Peter sat straight up seeming somewhat petrified, looking Rahlu right in the eye. Of course, Rahlu smiled back, waiting for this look on Peter's face.

When Rahlu stopped reeling and raised the rod high toward the shanty ceiling, out of the fishing hole popped Pete's lantern. Stanley also was quite impressed. He knew the object on the hook wasn't a fish, by the actions and hints from Rahlu, but he definitely never expected him to pull out that lantern.

Pete's face now was all bright eyes and as Rahlu told him, had a real shine. He couldn't care less about the look on his face, he got his lantern back. He didn't know what he was going to do when it came to telling his father that he'd knocked it in the hole. He only knew he would be done fishing for a long, long time. But now Peter felt a warm flow of relief in his body.

"Hey a flag's up!" Stanley said. "Pete, you stay here. We don't want to lose it in the hole."

There may even be a fish on it this time."

"Now, we have to think seriously about catching that fish. Stanley, you grab the gaff hook and Pete, grab the minnow bucket. Some hooks and a sinker, too, just in case," Rahlu told them.

The three of them stepped out of the shanty. Peter put the bait bucket down and turned around and made sure to lock the door. Rahlu and Stanley started out to the flagged tip-up at a faster, steady pace.

"What do you think we've got?" Stanley asked Rahlu. "We have caught many different types of fish through the ice in the past, and some were huge. Who knows what it may be."

"Don't get your hopes up yet," Rahlu replied. "First, we have to see if it didn't take the bait and leave us with a bare hook, empty handed. We don't know how long that flag's been tripped."

Once the two made their way to the tripped tip-up, Rahlu broke the ice that froze over the hole since Stanley set the tip-up at the start. When they slowly pulled the tip-up out of the hole there was no action or movement with the spool of fish line, nothing happening at all.

Peter came walking up to them and asked, "Well, what's the result?"

Both Rahlu and Stanley shook their heads. "I think we got stripped," Rahlu said, "Let me see the minnow bucket, Pete."

Just as Peter put the bucket down the spool started spinning swiftly as line unwrapped off the spool fast and continuously.

"Yee-hah!" Rahlu yelled. "We have something boys, and it's not small."

The two boys yelled, "YEAH," giving each other a punch on their shoulder.

As Rahlu continuously retrieved the line, bringing in their fish with patience for safe results, he said to the boys, "Watch out, don't step on the line lying around. This fish may make a run for it when it gets close to the hole. Stanley, get behind me with that gaff. I don't want to miss out on our chance to get this whopper out of the water."

After what seemed a long battle between Rahlu and the fish, back and forth, by the hole and, again and again, line whipping through the hole at remarkable speed, Rahlu decided that fish should be exhausted enough to give him a chance to gaff hook it and bring it up on the ice.

"OK, boys, get ready. I'm going to drag this monster out the next time I get it under us. Pete, get behind me and make sure the line is easy to take off without tangling up if I miss the thing. Stanley you get over there. As soon as I get it out, try to kick it back away from the hole, got it?" Both of the boys together nodded their heads, ready for whatever was about to take place.

Rahlu then put the gaff hook in the snow, at his convenience when he would need it. Slowly, he pulled the line out of the water, laying it so, if necessary, it could whip it back into the hole with the fish.

Finally, Rahlu could see the fish was just about close enough to attempt to land it. He kneeled down next to the hole, pulling out line until, suddenly, all in one smooth move, he grabbed the gaff, stuck it through the hole and seconds later that monster they had been fighting for quite some time was flopping on the ice between the three of them. Before it could even start flopping towards the hole, Stanley kicked it away.

Instantly, the three of them started hooting and hollering until finally, they were all hugging each other, in one big hug.

A couple minutes later, Rahlu grabbed the gaff hook and, hooking their trophy by the gills, dragged it back to the shanty. When they made sure they had brought everything back, even the tip-up, they got back in the shanty to calm down and get back to fishing.

Once they were inside, they all grabbed a cup and Stanley started pouring each a cup of coffee, definitely deserved. Not long after, they all felt somewhat relaxed and their heart rates were down to normal.

"That's one big sturgeon," Rahlu said. "I don't recall ever catching one even close to that size. Actually, nobody I know has ever come close. We'll have to talk to Victor?

About a half hour later, they noticed the day was about over and night-time was slowly moving into its place in Darquata.

After that, there wasn't any action in the shanty, so Rahlu and Stanley went out to retrieve the five tip-ups still set in the holes. At the same time, Pete collected everything inside the shanty to get ready to head back to town. Once he had everything packed and the inside of the shanty organized for the next opportunity to come out again, he doused out the small fire in the heater completely and headed out to the other guys.

"How are we going to do this, guys?" Rahlu asked the boys. "How about you two each grab a bucket of poles and tip-ups, and I'll grab the auger and the spud and the fish with the gaff?"

"Oh, the spud stays in the shanty, so my dad has it if he comes out without me," Pete said.

"OK, then I'll grab the fish and the auger." Rahlu added.

The three agreed with the plan and set out for shore. As they made their way back across the thin carpet of snow settled on the ice, once again, snow began falling lightly. In no time at all they were on shore and setting the buckets and equipment alongside the pillars on the dock at Isabella's.

When they walked into the front door of the restaurant, Peter nudged Stanley, catching Rahlu's attention also, and whispered, "Remember, don't mention anything about that lantern incident," making smiles on both of their faces.

CHAPTER 17

Seth and Catrina were just leaving Isabella's, walking down to the docks and talking along the way. They both noticed the frigid winds beginning to blow and whip the snowflakes around through the sky.

Catrina said, "This will be more delightful inside where it's nice, and warm. Why don't you come over to Staircase? I'd rather sit by the fireplace. This cold weather isn't for me. That fireplace will be more enjoyable. What do you think?"

"You don't need to ask me that," Seth replied.

"Follow me," Catrina said. She took off running away from the docks and across the park. Seth was right behind her, just about to the cobblestone road leading to the front door to Staircase when Catrina tripped in the snow drift and the two of them fell, disappearing into the bulk of the fresh snow bank.

As they got up out of the snow, the two walked to the sidewalk and tried brushing the snow off each other's coats. Then they turned and started walking, at a rapid pace, to make their way to the orphanage.

When they arrived at Staircase, they walked through the front door and Catrina said, "Oh, that feels nice. Go ahead, put your shoes on the mat, and I'll be right with you."

Seth removed his shoes and took off his coat. He looked at the staircase, impressed by all the details and designs perfectly carved into the dark, beautiful, cherry wood stairway leading to the upstairs level of an already immaculate home.

Catrina came walking through one doorway, with a tray and two mugs of steaming hot chocolate and said, "Follow me. We'll go sit in the living room." Then she added jokingly, "That's where the fireplace stands."

Seth remarked, "Can I ask you something?"

Catrina said, "Go ahead."

"Will you ever leave work? I mean, why are you still waiting on people? Sit down and take advantage of your time off. Get off your feet. Relax."

"I don't see any sense in sitting around doing nothing," Catrina replied. "If you would have known me when I was a kid, you'd probably realize how and why I am the way I am today."

"Catrina, I know everyone loves ALL that you do around here. They make it obvious. But give yourself some free time, too. For instance, I know I'm going to, very much, enjoy learning more about you, but it's your story. You don't need to apologize to anybody. It's your life, and your experiences. Should anyone look annoyed, show them the door," Seth told her, with a chuckle.

Catrina walked to the flowered love seat, and sat down next to Seth and gave him his mug. She started telling him about herself, and at the same time could feel the relief of having someone to tell it to. Someone she felt could actually hear all she had to say.

"To this day, I can only remember my mother and me coming to the big front door, here at Staircase, and the next thing that I can actually remember is Mother Adrian telling me everything she thought I should know about the place. From that time on, Mother Adrian has been my mother. I do all I can at Staircase, and at times, for any person that can use some help. That's where I should be."

With Seth's attention now focused on the real making of this girl he had just met, not too long ago, he could feel a loving feeling in all that she told him, putting a smile on his face.

Catrina then carried on, "After I was here for a long time, Mother Adrian began having me watch over Staircase while she ran errands. Father Gideon stopped by, now and then, but in time, I became Mother's only daughter. That's what I was told, anyway. Since then, there have been quite a few kids that have come and gone here at Staircase. I can remember people stopping in here with children. But, when I listened to the big door close on their way out, it was usually followed by a time span of pure sorrow as the children tried to follow their parents."

Catrina then stalled with her words to take a breath and wipe her eyes with her apron, still sitting on the arm of the loveseat.

Afterwards she continued. "As time went on, there have been many who have been left behind here at Staircase. Some of them I will never forget.

"First, there was Steve. He was the really smart one. Steve was a couple years older than me, 16 at that time. I liked him because anytime I needed an answer to almost anything, Steve knew what it was."

"Then there was Sabrina. I loved Sabrina. Catrina wiped her eyes again, but before she could begin saying anything more, Seth said, "Hey, look at me."

When he saw Catrina staring deep into his eyes, hurting, emotionally and sympathetically, the words that he was about to express vanished, leaving him wordless and tongue tied. He reached over to her and pulled her slowly to himself. With a hug, he held her firmly in his arms; something he had never done before. What started out as a story of Catrina's life was now beginning to manifest itself on Seth's heart as well, the beginning of a whole new story.

For a while, the two of them held each other tightly, possessing feelings neither of them knew. Both felt a comfort with confidence toward the actions they made. They held each other close, enjoying the love and companionship that they realized was there until Catrina sat up to maintain her composure, giving Seth a soft look with a warm smile, and started talking once again.

Sabrina was a newborn baby. A trapper found her at the entrance to the Talibaum Bridge, just outside of town. She was brought to Isabella, and Isabella brought Sabrina to Staircase. "To me, I can't see how someone can leave a newborn baby behind, just like that! I think anyone who leaves their newborn baby deserted, should never have brought the child into this world in the first place."

Catrina noticed she was getting worked up with anger, so she stopped telling her story and took a drink of her hot chocolate. She took a deep breath and then said, "Luckily, Dave and Joline took to Sabrina and gave her a new home. They live in Carsaria now. That's a small town a few miles down Arnagella's Trail. Sabrina is five now. Every time they come to Darquata, Sabrina visits Staircase. She's always hugging Mother and she looks at me like her big sister, I think. She and I will go walking around town and when other people remember her, it's all hugs and kisses. Everybody loves it. I'm just wondering how long before she gets tired of it all. Catrina smiled at Seth and the two both took a drink of hot chocolate.

Seth then said, "That's amazing!"

"Yes, I agree with that. It's good to know that a childlike Sabrina has a loving mother and father AND a real sound place to call home. Mother says Joline is expecting another little sister for Sabrina in the spring. I'm already looking forward to babysitting, again," Catrina said.

"Well, I have to say," Seth said, "from all I've learned about you, your place is at Staircase. I can already see you running this place."

"Yeah, well, I don't think I would want kids like Stanley and Tara under my wings. Because, in a matter of time, I'd either have two broken wings, or both of them will have broken necks. You do the math. Those two would even kill each other; I'm sure of it," Catrina finished.

The two of them both began laughing, trying to keep it quiet. Seth took a drink of hot chocolate and asked, "How long have the triplets been at Staircase?"

Catrina said, "Kevin, Kyle and Kimberly haven't been here too long, now. Just over a year. They were found in baskets under the picnic tables at the trail to Traders' Rendezvous. A trapper that comes every summer from Gymetaccos, named Dubonne' brought them all in on his back. Even Isabella got a kick out of that. Now, when he comes to town, Isabella tells him he's 'eating for free.' Still, Dubonne' slides a good chunk of money to the restaurant, every time he comes to town, in one way or another."

"Since the triplets arrived," she said, "there have been quite a few other children that have come and gone at Staircase. I can remember people dropping their children off at the front door and then just disappearing, as if their kids were some sort of delivery package. A few managed to show their faces a year or so later and take their children back. A couple times the really young ones didn't recognize their parents. That was truly pathetic to me."

Catrina's face was beginning to turn a light color red, and a look of anger. She took a drink of her hot chocolate, trying to forget the incident and let go of her emotions toward it.

"I can recall a few who spent a short time at Staircase," Catrina added, counting them on her fingers as she introduced them all to Seth.

"Let's see, now," she said, "first was Stew. Stew was the really quiet one. Unless he needed a question answered, or someone asked him a question, Stew never had much to say at all —ever! He was about my age; I think fifteen at the time. I liked Stew because if I wanted to get away from the noise and chaos of the younger kids, I would find Stew. He knew where and how to find quietness.

With a smile on her face, Catrina noticed Seth's cup was almost empty and she asked him, "Can I get you a refill on that hot chocolate?"

"Sure, if you don't mind," Seth replied.

"No problem. It's about time to make my rounds, anyway, checking up on the younger ones. I'll be back in just a minute," Catrina said as she got up and grabbed the cups to head to the kitchen.

"Wow!" Seth replied. "This town is like a big, happy bunch of friends, or should I say family? One way or another, this place does impress me."

Then he leaned toward Catrina and whispered, "Between you and me, this feels more like home than Dechnadi. It seems like we've been here for years."

After a split second of quiet, Catrina came out with a courageous comment, "Seth, you still haven't told me much about yourself and your brother Rahlu.

All I know is you said you're from Dechnadi. Just let me get these mugs refilled and then you can tell me your story."

Catrina picked up the tray and started her way to the kitchen for hot chocolate for both of them. Within minutes, she was back, giving a mug to Seth She sat down next to him in front of the warm fireplace.

Catrina said, "Do you have family back there, in Dechnadi? What type of town is Dechnadi? How big is the population? Are there any places in Dechnadi that you'd like to brag about? What is the…"

"WHOA" Seth interrupted Catrina abruptly. "First, I need a minute to get it all straight. That's too much at once. Let me think for a moment…" After a short pause, Seth picked up his cup, took a big gulp of his hot chocolate, cleared his throat and began.

"To start, my father was a well-known ship builder of Dechnadi. He and the people he hired helped to make many ships that are used in the fishing industry today, all over, not just in Dechnadi. If you were to look at the base of the mast of a ship, even in the Port of Darquata, and you found the initials DWS, that's proof that my father built it. Those initials stand for Dameon Willord Ship-builders. The company has been in business for 115 years. My grandfather's father, my great-grandfather, started it all and it's been handed down from generation to generation."

"Now that's something to be proud of!" Catrina said. "How long have you and Rahlu been working with it?"

Seth, quietly replied, "We're not."

Catrina, startled to hear such a reply, asked, "Why not?"

Seth replied, as he stared down into his cup, "Neither of us have any interest. We both make our livings on the boats, from doing the nets and the intake for that voyage. Most of the time, you're not only doing one job on your trip. By the time the quota of fish is met, you've done every position on the ship; truthfully, building the ships doesn't even interest me. Rahlu will have to give you his reason. As for me, I'd rather be fishing—literally."

Catrina got the pun to his reply and both of them laughed. Then, without hesitation, she reached out, gave him a hug, followed by a kiss on the cheek.

Seth's eyes were opened wide, trying to regain the feelings that seemed numb by the actions that just took place. Emotionally, everything seemed like heaven to him.

Privately, Catrina couldn't believe what she had just done. Blushing extremely, she looked at Seth, who seemed to experience a supernatural atmosphere of his own. She had no clue what was now going through his mind, but wanted more than ever to find out his personal thoughts to her actions.

She only hoped she didn't ruin her chances to make something of the feelings she had for him. She only asked herself, silently, "What just happened?"

Suddenly, to her surprise, Seth reached out, softly grabbed her arm and pulled her closer to him. He placed a long, warm and, to him, definitely deserved kiss on her lips, sending feelings through her body she never knew existed.

At that moment, something came over Catrina. Something she never felt or experienced before, in all her time at Staircase. It was unordinary, in a way, and kind of embarrassing to her, too, until an impulse of panic came over her completely.

"I need to go check on those kids," she said, as she got up off the loveseat. "I'll talk to you later, OK?" And she was up and heading to the kitchen before Seth had a chance to say, "Sure thing."

And then she was gone. Just like that.

CHAPTER 18

As Seth walked his way to Traders' Rendezvous, he was stumped. First, he was enjoying Catrina's companionship. It didn't seem like meeting someone new. To him, Catrina seemed like someone he'd known for years. Now she was gone. No reason at all. Did he do something, or even say something wrong? If so, what was it?

That night, after what seemed like a nice, sunny winter day, winter now was moving in, punching Darquata with a seasonal eye-opener; a ferocious cold front that brought with it ten to thirty-foot waves over the break walls on the Meskipit Sea. Raging wind and pounding waves, potent enough together, made howling rumbles that lasted throughout the night, freezing a heavy layer of ice, with a generous amount of snow over everything. That, in the early morning, made some exercise for all the shipmates docked in Darquata.

Early the next morning, Seth and Rahlu were bringing in wood for the Inn's fire places and kitchen stoves. As they made their way through the freshly fallen snow, Seth just couldn't keep from thinking about that incident between Catrina and him the night before. She seemed like an important part of his life, now, and he wasn't about to let her go.

"C'mon kid," Rahlu said, trying to hurry little brother up. "The tips of my fingers are getting numb. I want to get done here and go down to Isabella's to talk to some of those old 'coots' that sit at the corner table.

I'm thinking we could work for somebody this spring, as a deckhand on one of their boats or helping out around here in the boatyards. As you can see by now, bro, I can't take this much longer; day to day boredom. I'm going to go mad!"

Rahlu swung the axe he was using, chopping a bigger piece of firewood down to usable size.

Seth smiled toward his brother's actions, as he loaded up his arms with blocks of the recently chopped wood and started heading to the back door of the inn. As he walked in the inside door, he heard Beth say, "That's enough, you two; leave something for our son to do. You boys make it too easy for that kid."

"Oh, that's OK, ma'am," Seth said. "I, myself, have to keep busy.

I was thinking of maybe helping out Isabella or doing something like that."

"Oh, that's sweet. Mother Adrian could always use some help, somewhere in or around Staircase," Beth replied.

Instantly, Seth's eyes widened, like a light electric shock had just connected inside him.

"That's it!" Seth thought to himself. He would offer his help at Staircase. He could spend more time around Catrina and, eventually, find just what kept her from opening up to him. That's what he was going to do. He dried his hands and had a cup of coffee while talking to Beth. Seth asked her to tell Rahlu where he was heading.

Minutes later, Seth was trekking across the snow drifts in a hurry to get to his new job, as he called it. His next stop was Isabella's to have a morning coffee and think about how he was going to present himself and his idea to Mother Adrian.

As he walked into the front door of the restaurant, he was greeted with a variety of 'hellos' from the many elder ship captains and Vic and Crendon. Seth told everybody good morning and made his way to the designated table where he and Rahlu were known to sit.

Isabella met him at the table and poured him a cup of coffee, put the pot on the table and pulled out her note pad to take his order.

"Good morning, Seth. How's your morning started, today?" Isabella asked.

"Oh, I'd rather be sitting here looking out at the green leaves, regardless of the sun shining. Anything but this snow would be fine by me," he answered.

"I agree with you there," Isabella told him.

"Too bad I can't change it with a snap of my fingers.
I'd prefer the warmer weather anytime."

Seth cracked a smile but didn't say another word. Isabella sensed there was some sort of static in the situation between him and Catrina and was a little 'antsy' herself trying to find out the story without too much aggravation.

"What can I get you this morning, young man?" she asked him.

"Oh, I'm not really hungry this morning, Isabella," Seth told her.

"Now listen. We've been through this before. I hope you're not going to make me pull rank on you again. You've got to eat something. How 'bout I get you an order of toast?"

"OK, I'm not going to argue with you. How's an order of raisin toast?" Seth replied.

"I'm sorry, we don't have raisin toast," Isabella replied, to his surprise. "I'm just joking," she added,

"Raisin toast it is." She cracked him a smile and then said, "Smile, make the day a little brighter."

Isabella turned and headed toward the kitchen.

She was determined to figure how to get some info out of him about the couple.

When Isabella returned with Seth's raisin toast, she couldn't be discrete about it any longer. She put the small plate on his table, sat down across from him and asked him, "So, how was the afternoon with Catrina at Staircase."

With no hesitation at all, Seth responded, "I really don't know. At first, the three kids, Kevin, Kyle and Kimberly came running out of the dining room and gave me hugs. After that, she just had to serve me coffee or hot chocolate. I swear that girl goes above and beyond to serve everybody but herself. Anyway, she told me how and when she entered Staircase and the other residents that had come and gone since she came. She made a pretty complete and detailed description of her past with Mother Adrian and even a few things about you."

Isabella could see Seth's expression on his face and replied, "Yeah, nice try young man. You still don't know who you're talking to, huh." She gave him a smile and then added, "Tell me more."

He continued, "We made our way into the living room and sat down on the sofa in front of the fireplace. She wanted to know more about me, so I told her of my growing up in Dechnadi and how I, nor Rahlu, feel we have to be the ones to carry on the business of our father, making ships and boat pieces needed to make a ship complete. I told her my whole life story, which wasn't really much to tell. The next thing I remember I said, "Promise me you won't tell Rahlu, because I'll never hear the end of it..."

"Don't worry. This is as far as your story goes," Isabella told him.

"OK," Seth said, "Things got real quiet until, out of the blue, she gave me a big hug, then a kiss. Now, something like that never happened to me before. I felt something I never experienced before. I didn't know what I should do. So, I reached over and brought her close enough to me to give her a kiss, too. That's when the whole evening ended. She told me she had to go check on the kids, or something like that. The next thing I remember is walking through the snow back to Traders' Rendez-vous. Trying to figure out just what I did wrong."

"Oh, Seth, don't worry. You didn't do anything wrong. You said it all seemed like something new to you. Well, let me tell you, it's all something new to Catrina, too. I'll guarantee it. But you don't tell her I told you, either...Deal?"

Seth shook hands with Isabella, saying, "It's a deal."

Isabella then said, "Just give her some time. Both of you are still kids, in many ways, and when the right time comes you both will know if you are meant to be. If not, you both will feel glad that you found out together. But I have a feeling that you two will cherish having each other; just you wait and see. Remember —Hush!"

CHAPTER 19

Early the next morning, Seth and Rahlu began the usual chores they felt were their way of paying their debts to Ian and Beth, who had over and over, told them not to worry about it. Still, was a 'must' for the two of them.

While Rahlu was digging out firewood, covered by another four inches of freshly fallen snow, Seth was pounding on the wood to break it apart, stack it on the sled and take it into the shed on the back of the Inn to let it thaw before it was actually needed. After they completed the tasks at hand, the two of them decided to head to Isabella's and have their morning coffee and visit with the traders, ship captains, and crew members.

As they made their way to town, Seth, unexpectedly said, "I want to tell someone, now."

"What?" Rahlu replied.

"I feel it's time to tell everyone interested about what happened. You know, about our experience and about Skelly and everybody else. I think I might feel better just letting someone else know. I would really like to tell someone about it," Seth said. "Do you think I should?"

"Little brother, that's up to you. If you think it will help you feel better, then, by all means, go ahead," Rahlu told him. "Truthfully, I'll probably share some of my input, too. I tell you what, once we get done eating, we'll go sit at that corner table and let the big guy know we have something to tell them. I'm sure we will be more than welcomed. I know they've been waiting to hear this for quite some time, probably since we arrived." "OK, let's do it," Seth said, more than willingly.

Minutes later, Seth and Rahlu entered the front door of Isabella's and again, went right to what seemed to be their table. They sat down and seconds later Kevin, Kyle, and Kimberly came running to them and got up on the benches to give them both a morning hug. The two brothers looked at each other and couldn't keep from smiling. "Good morning to each of you, too," Rahlu said, with a touch of sarcasm

Catrina came out of the kitchen and said, "You three go play somewhere else. Leave the two men alone. I'm sure they won't forget about you…believe me"

"Good morning, you two, she said. "What can I get you this fine day?"

Rahlu said, "I'll take two eggs, toast and coffee. What do you want, little brother?"

Seth's eyes were magnetized on Catrina. He recalled a little of the chat with Isabella and somehow squeaked out, "Surprise me."

Catching her by surprise also, Catrina almost stuttered when she asked, "How about the Special?"

"That'll be great," Seth replied.

"Good. I'll be right back with your coffee," she said.

Rahlu got up to leave the table saying, "Be right back. I've got to use the men's room."

Seth sat by himself, in his own world, wondering what to say to Catrina, next time she came to the table. He didn't want to say anything that would make things seem more awkward than they were already, but he didn't want to miss her more than he did already, either.

Catrina came to the table and wordlessly poured Seth a cup of coffee. She was just about to turn to leave, when she turned to look at him and spontaneously the two of them said, "I'm sorry."

Together, they started laughing.

Rahlu came walking up to the table asking, "OK, what's so funny? Are you talking about me?"

"No, believe me, we're NOT talking about you," Seth said sarcastically. Then he asked Catrina, "How about I meet you here when you're finished working?"

"That sounds perfect," Catrina told him. "Let me go see if your breakfasts are ready," she said as she turned and walked away.

"Well, look at that," Rahlu said, teasing Seth to the maximum irritation on the nerves. "Little Bro found himself a 'squeeze.'"

"Shut up, Rahlu!" Seth replied, "And don't say anything like that when she's around, either!"

"Oh, calm down Seth. I'm glad to see you've met someone to be with. It's easy to see she likes being with you. Who knows, she just might be the one you need to talk to, psychologically speaking."

"Maybe, but I still want to talk to Victor and Crendon. They know what I'm talking about and know how to relate to it. Besides, we do have to start thinking what to do about Skelly. He deserves a better departure."

"It's called a funeral, little brother," Rahlu said, smiling. "Besides I've been thinking about that, all along. I figured to talk to Victor about him before warmer weather starts rolling in, before he starts to ripen, anyway."

Just then, Mother Adrian came into the big door followed by Tara and Claire, who were assisting her grandmother, Martha Pepper, too. Once the two girls got Martha into the restaurant, she said, "I thank you both for helping me get through that cold to get here, but I think I should know my way around this place. Thank you, once again, but I'll take it from here."

Claire and Tara looked at each other, a little puzzled. Hearing something like that coming from Martha's mouth was surprising.

"Claire, my dear, I was coming to Isabella's even before you were a twinkle in your father's eye," Martha said. Knowing it would take a second for the joke to sink in Martha made her way to one of the counter stools and said, "Isabella, I'm here! Give me my usual, hey?"

Still kind of flustered by those remarks and the actions, as well, Tara and Claire turned and looked at Mother. Mother just smiled and said, "Why don't the two of you go see if Isabella needs some help in the kitchen. Tara, I don't want to hear you making trouble for Stanley, either. That boy has been here since six o'clock this morning. Show him a little respect or I'll arrange some reservations for you in the dish room, if you wish."

"Don't worry, Mother," Tara replied, "He's isn't worth that much."

When they went into the kitchen Stanley saw Claire and dropped all he was doing to give her a hug. Then Claire kissed him on the cheek.

"Gross, you two need to get a room!" Tara told them, as she turned around and headed right back to the dining room.

"How much longer are you working? Grandma said her evening is planned to visit here for awhile," Claire said.

Stanley replied, "I have no clue. It seems that things are just starting to slow down. Who knows what those old turkeys are going to order, out of the blue.

Why don't you go out and keep your grandma company, or out of trouble. Those 'geezers' will probably be hitting on her soon."

"True. But you really don't know grandma. She'll love it. She's an old lady, but, believe me, she'll definitely be a run for their money," Claire said.

Stanley just snickered. Claire stepped up to him, again, gave him a kiss on the cheek and stepped out into the dining room. Stanley turned around and headed to the stairwell to the basement. He knew the faster he had everything prepped for morning, the more time he'd have for Claire, and THAT put some light in his evening outlook.

CHAPTER 20

Back at Seth and Rahlu's table, the two were just getting finished eating, when Catrina returned with more coffee.

"Sure, I'll take some more of that," Rahlu said as he lifted his cup to her. Then he said, "You two have fun. I'm going to talk to Victor and let him know the plan we had."

Catrina looked at Seth, puzzled. He just said, "Don't mind my brother. He needs help, believe me."

The two were just starting to talk when Rahlu yelled, "Hey Seth, come here. These men want to talk to you."

Seth told Catrina, "That's my cue. The two of us decided we would let these guys know all that happened onboard the ship and how we ended up here, in Darquata. I am planning to walk you home after work, so wait for me, OK?"

"Don't worry, you're not getting out of it," Catrina told him, as she started walking to the kitchen.

Seth stood up and walked to the corner table where Rahlu was sitting with Victor, Crendon and Jed, Mr. Solgood and another captain, Marcus of the 'Leveda'. When he got to the table, Victor stood up and shook hands with the boy, saying, "Your brother was telling me you wanted to talk about something. Go ahead, have a seat. I'll be right back. I gotta use the 'head.' Oh, and don't let the big guy scare you away. The kids already have him trained."Crendon and Mr. Solgood both smiled.

It didn't take long for Seth and Rahlu to feel comfortable, when Crendon asked, "How long were you two working on that boat?"

Rahlu responded, "I was on the ship for just about a year when 'little brother' here decided he should join me, too. Even though our father has a business making ships and parts as well, we both thought there was more out there for the two of us. Other family members would be more than glad to carry on the family tradition. It's been in the family for about one-hundred and fifteen years. If you look at the base of the ship's mast and find DWS imprinted in the steel plate, that ship was made by our family, one generation through the years, anyway."

Jed Solgood asked, "What does the DWS stand for?"

Marcus told him, "Dameon Willard Ship-builders. Actually, there are quite a few on the waters today or in the harbors this time of year."

Just then, Victor came walking up to the table and sat down. He looked at Seth and said, "OK, we all want to know about your journey to Darquata. First, we only want to hear what you want to tell us. We don't want to make it hard for you two, and we definitely are not trying to push it. You tell us the way you feel is right. So, that being said, you can begin whenever you're comfortable."

Seth began to tell his memory of their drastic experiences that all started onboard the ship they were working for, the Palatina.

"To me," he said, "the whole thing started when I was in our sleeping quarters. I just got through putting in my time on deck, evening shift. I do know I was sound asleep and relaxed. That's when this 'loving' brother of mine woke me up." Seth looked at Rahlu and cracked a smile, knowing the smart remark was, someday, going to get back to him. He knew Rahlu.

He continued the story. "Rahlu started yelling, 'Get up! C'mon hurry up. Something's wrong on deck. Seth let's go! C'mon little brother, get dressed, we've got to go!'"

"At that time, I noticed the ship's emergency horn on deck was howling. I got up and put on my clothes and boots and grabbed my jacket and hat and gloves. Rahlu and I started running down the hall, heading for the ladder that would take us quickly out the door and on-deck with most everyone else onboard.

Suddenly, I felt the whole ship tilt, as did everyone else, of course. I lost my balance and it knocked me off my feet."

Seth paused for a moment, looking his brother straight in the eye, as if to ask if he was telling them the right story. Rahlu smiled at little brother and nodded his head.

Little brother continued. "The next thing I know, Connor and Zylla, two more crew members, were handing out life jackets. Rahlu ran over and began disconnecting life rafts, while Townsend and Skelly started inflating them as fast as they could. Within minutes, they had all five of them ready, for everybody. That's when Captain Conway and first-mate Fraiser came running down from Captain's Quarters. Both had on their life jackets and anxiously headed toward the rest of us. When everyone was ready to get off the ship, the captain told us that the ship, "ran upon a sand bar as something punctured the bow of the ship and at this very moment the ship's sinking at a fast, steady rate."

Seth took a deep breath, and then continued, "Captain then told everyone to start unloading those rafts…Skelly and Zylla, were first.'"

"We didn't take long to get off the ship, but Captain and Fraiser were the last to get into a raft. Minutes later, I remember looking back toward the position of the ship. It was gone. But what really startled me was the raft with Captain Conway and Fraiser. They seemed to have disappeared. At that point we all knew to get far away from the location where the ship went down. As far away as possible."

Victor and Crendon both took a look around the room. Everyone in Isabella's at that time was quietly frozen in time. All were anticipating the next part of the story, with stunned looks on their faces, not knowing what was to be the final approach. Victor noticed Isabella motioning to him to meet her in the kitchen. He, also, noticed that Isabella had that specific look on her face; the one that meant, 'I mean NOW!'

As Victor left the table, Seth, too, got up and headed to the restroom.

When Seth walked into the restroom, he started the water running, both hot and cold faucets, trying to hide the crying sounds that were coming from deep inside him. He turned around and sat down on the toilet seat trying to muffle his emotions and keep from publicly being heard. Still, he just couldn't stop. Just the memory of their experience was emotionally tearing him apart. He still couldn't get over the incidence he woke up to.

Seth began thinking to himself, "Where would I be now, if it wasn't for Rahlu? Better yet, why was it me that didn't go down with the ship?"

Seconds later, Seth was crying again, loudly, and this time realized it more. He stood up, flushed the toilet to help silence his sense of disgrace. He stepped toward the sink and found himself looking in the mirror, noticing the sad look those tears had left upon his face. He put his hands under the cold water and began washing his face and trying to cool himself.

When he dried his face and hands with a towel, he could tell he was beginning to calm down. He now could feel a bit more confident in himself. So, he unlocked the door, stepped out into the hallway and headed toward the dining room. He knew there were people waiting to hear more of the story.

Seth came walking out, head down, feeling quite embarrassed and went straight to the corner table, where Rahlu and Crendon and Marcus were sitting. When he sat down, Rahlu put his arm around little brother and gave him a manly hug, tight and positive, with a little shake of confidence. Seth looked at his big brother, and knowing he was on his side, showed him a somewhat smiling expression. As he looked across the table, he noticed Crendon looking at him, too, with a caring look on his face.

In the kitchen, Isabella instantly asked Victor, "Are you out of your mind? Do you really think those young kids should be listening to this? It's not like one of your stories, you know. This is a true story, a true 'legit' experience. Who knows what could be going through the heads of those little ones, or even how are they to react?"

Victor stopped her there with a louder, firmer voice saying, "Bella stop! This is something real, a step by step detailed story of an adventure that has no other ending. A true adventure; true description, true survivors. Their feelings and after-effects they're now trying to manage, themselves. It's like a therapy to the brothers and an introduction to the true world of the seas for the kids. They'll be alright, believe me."

Victor stepped closer to Isabella and offered a hug. She leaned toward him and Victor made it a big sincere hug. He then gave her a sweet kiss on the cheek and told her, "I'm going back out there. I need to know just what happened. When you come out, you come and sit by me." Victor smiled and gave her another loving kiss on the cheek.

Then, from across the room they heard, "Awe, isn't that special?"

The two of them, somewhat startled, turned to look toward the voice.

There stood Stanley, watching the whole thing, looking at the two with a "shitty" looking grin on his face. "That looks so sweet" he added, sarcastically.

"Get out of here," Isabella told him. "Get out there and listen...you just might learn something!"

Stanley walked by heading to the door of the dining room while Isabella kept trying to snap him with the towel she had in her hand.

Victor and Isabella looked at each other. Victor with a big grin, himself, was trying hard to keep from laughing. Isabella instantly snapped him and Victor went racing out the dining room door. As Isabella stood there, she, too, had a big smile on her face; thinking, "Damn that kid!"

For a short time, the whole restaurant could have heard a pin hit the floor. It seemed like nobody was even breathing as Seth began preparing himself to continue.

"Did you see any whales?" a four-year-old boy yelled from across the room.

Everyone chuckled. Seth turned around and, with a smile, looked at the curious, yet innocent boy. "No, unfortunately. I would have loved to though."

The boy's mother motioned for him to come and sit by her. As the boy started toward his mother, Seth told her, "That's OK He's just a boy. They should be asking questions."

Victor said, "Zachary, why don't you come over here?"

The little boy nervously started toward the corner table, turning around in his tracks to make sure of his mother's approval.

"C'mon. You come over here and sit by the 'big men's' table. You can sit by me."

Little Zachary, with more determination, picked up pace to get to Vic's table and when he got to the table, Victor stood up and said, "Go ahead, get right up there, between me and Crendon."

Zachary hopped up on the bench, standing for a few seconds, until Victor sat back down and put him on his lap. Zachary was all smiles. After seeing the bright smiley face of that curious little boy, Seth was all smiles, too. Once Zachary was seated, everyone in Isabella's put their attention toward Seth's story.

He began again. "Truthfully, the next thing I remember is waking up on the raft, on the beach. When I actually had my bearings straight, I first noticed some of the ship's equipment rolling around at the edge of the water. So, I got up to go collect what I could. That's when I noticed Rahlu pulling Skelly out of the water. Immediately, I ran over to help.

We pulled him away from the water's edge, out of the mist that blew along the beach with the northwesterly winds. In a couple of minutes we found a somewhat secluded area and laid Skelly on a flat boulder, trying to get him to relax. We both knew he was suffering from pain, severely."

Zachary asked, "What does that mean…sa-vere-ly?"

Seth looked at him in the eye and, with a smile, told him, "That means real, real bad."

Zachary turned and looked at Victor with a serious expression on his face and asked him, "Did you know that?"

Everyone again had to laugh. Zachary couldn't figure what it was they were laughing about, but he just smiled.

"Yes Zach, I know what that means," Victor replied. "Now, shh, let's let him tell his story, OK?"

Victor looked across the dining room to see Isabella trying to hide her laughing, and he cracked a smile himself to the kid's reply.

"Anyway," Seth said, "When we finally got Skelly somewhat calmed down, Rahlu insisted I go back and try to find as much as I could that might be helpful. Luckily, when I got down to the water, I spotted our emergency medics bag floating about twenty feet out. So, I jumped in and waded out to grab it as fast as I could, even though I knew the outcome.

"When I got the bag I ran as fast as I could back to Rahlu and Skelly and immediately opened the bag to treat Skelly's injuries. When I attempted to hand the things necessary to Rahlu, I saw that look on Rahlu's face. One expression I hope to never see again; never!"

"Rahlu looked at me, staring me right in the eye for a couple seconds and then shook his head. That was the end of Skelly," Seth said, working hard to keep from crying again.

That's when a soft voice spoke up with a lovable tone asking, "Can I give anyone some more coffee?" Even Isabella, from way across the room, heard that, clearly.

Seth's experience was now starting to affect Catrina's emotions. She poured fresh coffee into all the cups on the table. Then she looked at Seth, trying not to express just how his story was making her want to break down and cry. Catrina turned, and at a faster pace headed straight toward the kitchen.

When Catrina made her way back into the kitchen, she put the coffee pot on the stove and walked to the counter. Seconds later, Isabella entered only to find Catrina sniffling, with her head held low, lines of tears running down her face.

"Please excuse me Catrina," Isabella begged.

Catrina turned surprised to see Isabella standing right there inside the kitchen door. She wiped her eyes in her apron and replied, "What?"

"I'm sorry honey," Isabella said. "I can see how much that man means to you, and you know it, too. Anyone can see it on your face."

"Isabella, why does this hurt, so bad?" Catrina cried, as she ran to her and buried her face into Isabella's chest, with an extremely tight hug. Isabella, in return, hugged Catrina dearly, knowing something like this was bound to happen, eventually, and inevitably.

CHAPTER 21

At the corner table, Seth started once again; "Rahlu and I had to think for a couple minutes on what to do with Skelly. We finally decided to wrap him in a ripped piece of the rubber raft that was beached not far down the shoreline. It took us some time to find something to cut the raft with for enough material to wrap Skelly. We were still trying to find something sharp to cut the raft when Rahlu called and said he found something that would work. When I got up to Rahlu he said, "I'll be damned!"

Rahlu interrupted his little brother. "Seth, you forgot, there are kids listening. Let me continue."

Rahlu started to tell his side of the story, but before he began, having consideration for the purpose the story was even being told, he looked at his little brother and said, "Unless you want to."

Seth said, "Go ahead. I need to take a break."

Rahlu gave his brother a quick hug and began; "Anyway, what he was telling you, I was pulling Skelly off the boulder to search his pockets. That's when I said what Seth said. Searching the pockets I luckily found Skelly's pocket knife. After the discovery, we cut a generous size off the raft material and wrapped Skelly tightly. We used the rest of the raft material to drag him with us as we traveled along the beach."

"After what seemed to be at least a half of a day, a long, long time, both of us had to take a break. The winds were getting stronger and stronger, straight from the North. We felt as if they were cutting into our faces. So, we left Skelly laying and raced to the bottom of the cliffs looking for some secluded, hide-away place to get some cover and protection from the strong winds. Believe me, it wasn't easy."

"The traveling started getting shorter time between rests. Dragging Skelly was taking its toll on the two of us," Rahlu said. "Then unexpectedly, when we took another break, we got to the bottom of the cliffs out of the winds and noticed what looked like a small 'cubby-hole' behind a big size boulder. When we went to check it out, we were surprised to find the 'cubby-hole was a cave and a huge one, at that. So, cautiously, we went inside, praying there wasn't already something else calling it 'home.'

Rahlu paused to take a gulp of his coffee. Under the table, he lightly kicked Victor and then rolled his eyes toward Zachary, who was tensely, deep in his imagination.

Rahlu smiled and started telling an unrelated, 'scary' story.

"When we went into the cave, way back, and i was getting darker, we thought we saw EYES….."

Victor shook his leg, the one Zachary was sitting on and loudly said, "BOO!"

Little Zachary's reaction made the little man jump so high he ended up on the bench between Victor and Crendon. Crendon's reaction made him grab the back of Zachary's shirt to keep him from falling under the table. Once again, people in the restaurant began to laugh, trying not to be heard by the young boy, who was already aware that the joke was on him. He started to break down in tears from the embarrassment. Then, over every other voice in the building, the people heard a stunning,

"Victor!!" Isabella yelled. "That's enough! Zachary, if you want to go sit by your mother, you go ahead. Those men at that table are only trouble."

"Oh, leave the poor boy alone. We were only having fun, right Zach? Victor replied. "Are you ready to hear some more of the story?"

Zachary wiped his eyes, and his nose, and nodded his head. Then he said, "Yeah, I want to hear some more."

Victor said, "Alright. We promise we won't do that anymore, OK?"

Again, the little boy nodded his head, waiting for Rahlu to start telling the rest of the story.

At the counter by the entrance into the kitchen, Isabella was staring into Victor's eyes, sternly, shaking her head; and her fist. Victor's facial expression was just a smirk as he rolled his eyes to her. Isabella turned and went into the kitchen with a temper. She came out a few seconds later with a coffee pot in her hand and made her rounds filling cups for everyone in the restaurant. When she finally got to the corner table, Isabella poured coffee into all the cups but Victor's.

Victor asked, "Hey Darling, what about me?"

Isabella instantly replied, "Do you think you DESERVE it?" She looked at him, and reluctantly filled his cup. As she turned and started walking away from the men, Isabella then said, "Next time, you'll be wearing it." The whole house got a 'kick' out of her reply, even Victor and Zachary laughed.

"We went as far back into the cave as we could," Rahlu continued. We were far enough to where the winds were only a howling sound to us. We both were totally exhausted and just sat down next to each other to try to feel the warmth and, truthfully, the place began to feel quite comfortable to me, compared to what exertion we'd been putting ourselves through to survive. The next thing I remember is Seth and his LOUD snoring; and believe me little brother, THAT is no joke," Rahlu finished, with a smile.

Seth replied, "You have no room to talk big brother. Besides, what do you think woke me up? To be honest, I was just glad we got some sleep. But once the two of us were up and pretty much ready to continue our trek down the beach, the real decision was what to do with Skelly?"

He paused a moment to take a drink of coffee. Then he went on. "After discussing the next step, we decided it would be most appropriate to leave him in the cave and come back for him after we got ourselves some help, before it was too late. We figured that even though the temperature in the cave was feeling somewhat comfortable for our own bodies, the actual temperature was way below that stage for Skelly's body to decompose. So, when the two of us felt rested and ready to move on, we made a quick dash to get Skelly and bring him back as fast as possible."

Rahlu reached across the table to Zachary and tapped him on his arm saying, "Is this still sounding interesting?"

In an instant, Zachary replied, "Yeah, but what is dee-cum...decu-posh...you know!

Victor asked Zachary, "Do you mean decomposure?"

"Yeah, that," he said.

"OH, that's not important right now. We'll talk about that later," Victor told him. "First, let's hear some more of the story."

"OK" Zachary said.

Crendon spoke up and asked them, "About how long were you two in the cave and how long before you noticed the day turning to night? Do you have any ideas of how much time was spent in the cave? And, one more thing, what was Skelly's condition when you got him in the cave?"

"First, it wasn't long at all and the daylight began fading, quickly, I might add. But neither of us would pass up the chance to get some more sleep. It was definitely needed. As far as Skelly, we figured if we were going to spend the night, we may as well leave him out there in the cold. Of course, we did put him just outside the entrance of the cave, in case of any starving critters or, especially, seahawks. We did leave him wrapped, for a better preservation and to keep every part of him that was frozen to remain at that," Rahlu said.

"We even wrapped him one more time for less chance of any critters to get a bite," Seth added sarcastically, with a smile

"How did you two see anything in the cave at nighttime?" asked a female voice.

To the men's surprise, Catrina had come out of the kitchen and sat with the younger children just a couple tables away. In due time, she found herself wanting to get closer and closer to Seth. She could feel the new, mysterious feeling she had for him again, getting stronger than she ever imagined. But she did feel like she had to be there next to him.

As for Seth, when he heard Catrina's voice, from right behind him, he turned around. When he looked into Catrina's eyes, the whole atmosphere lit up again and the feelings he was struggling with for the last couple of hours seemed to have evaporated. Isabella could see it on his face, too. Evidently, the two meant much more to each other than either of them was aware of and Isabella was going to help, in more ways than one.

"It was just before daybreak when we started getting ready to continue down the shoreline to find help," Rahlu told everyone. "That's when I told Seth to stop everything and be quiet. I heard something growl from deeper in the cave."

Rahlu, again, looked at Zachary with that serious look. But this time Zachary was on to him when Rahlu said, "It was just Seth's belly."

Zachary let out a loud, child type laugh from deep inside. Everyone else got a good laugh, too.

Then Seth leaned toward Zachary and at a low voice told him, "He should be glad it wasn't a fart!"

The young boy laughed even harder as so did the rest of the men at the table.

Then Rahlu continued, "We decided to leave Skelly in the cave, wrapped in the raft material and put him where the cold winds blew into the cave's entrance, to keep him cold as long as possible, hoping some high tide didn't sweep him away, out to sea."

Rahlu paused, took another drink of coffee and said to Seth, "Go ahead, little bro' you can take it from here."

Seth took a moment to think back, then started, saying, "The next thing I remember is, we decided to roll a few bigger sized boulders out on the beach and stack them as tall as possible so that they would be noticeable when we go looking for him in the spring, or maybe sooner, depending on the winter weather. Once we got the 'marker' in a recognizable location, we began the final stretch of our journey along the shoreline. From then on, we did nothing but walk as fast and as far as we could. Lucky for us, the winds were blowing from the north/northwest and that was directly behind us, more bearable than blowing into our faces."

Just then, the front door of the restaurant opened with a big gust of cold winds whipping into the place. Everyone noticed a small group of the ship mates walk in.

"Close that damn door!" Martha Pepper yelled.

"Martha!" Isabella said sternly, "That wasn't necessary."

"Well, I just wish those boys had some common sense," Martha said.

Isabella just looked to the men and shook her head with a little sarcasm, and a smile.

It was the crew members of Marcus' ship, Leveda, Dan, Al, Big Jim and Little John. They all walked over and sat down at the table adjacent to the corner table, or as Catrina called it, the "Turkey Coop." Seconds later, the big door opened again.

Martha, sitting with her back to the door, spun around on the stool she was sitting on, at the counter, saying, "I said close that...Oh, it's just you."

She didn't realize it was Ralph, the crew leader aboard the Leveda, Crendon's 'big' brother.

"Well, a pleasant hello to you, too," he told her.

"You need to teach your kids how to..."Martha was about to say, when she was unexpectedly interrupted.

"Oh, quit your bickering, woman," Ralph told Martha with a smile, "Before I put you over my knee!"

He then looked to Victor and said, "See, I told you that woman's a bad influence."

Victor and everyone at the table, even little Zachary, all cracked a smile. Martha, of course, quieted down, after yelling to Isabella, "Sis, bring me another."

Ralph, standing at his crew's table, looked right at Little John and said, "Move over Shorty and let me sit down."

Instantly, everyone at the table shifted their positions and Ralph sat down facing Victor's table. He said, "Hey, Salty Dog, what's the stinky fish story for me, today?"

"Actually," Victor replied, "I want you to meet these guys; the bigger one's Rahlu and his little brother, Seth. Evidently, these two are the last soul survivors from aboard the Palatina, a ship previously from Dechnadi."

Ralph then looked at Rahlu and asked, "Wasn't that Conway's rig?"

Rahlu quietly replied, "I hate to say it, but, yes."

"Oh, wow! Conway was a damn good captain. I can't believe the Palatina went down. I did like that guy. That's very heartbreaking to hear," Ralph expressed. He then added, "Besides, he owes me money from last month's poker table."

Isabel la just shook her head and turned to walk into the kitchen, thinking to herself, "None of those men have any respect."

After a few more introductions and updating the newcomers on Seth and Rahlu's adventure, all the attention was back to Rahlu as he began discussing the final leg of their journey to Darquata.

"Once we began to see the beaming light from the town's lighthouse, we started to pick up the pace in getting here. By the time we got to the edge of town, I was struggling to keep myself moving while trying to keep Little Brother on his feet as well. That's when I saw Stanley walking down the cobblestone road by the harbor. Thanks to Stanley, that was the last of our struggle with survival."

"Yes," Seth added, "and from that moment, for me, it's like being introduced to a whole new world. Of course, it's a reality check in some ways, but it's a difference in the 'ordinary' ways back in Dechnadi. And for me, it's given me a better idea of just what my purpose in life may be."

As Seth finished his final input to their journey, Isabella came back out of the kitchen and, after hearing everything he had just said to the crowd, looked at him, eye to eye, with a sweet smile, as if to say, 'that was impressive.'

Isabella walked over to Seth and whispered something into his ear, and in a split-second Seth looked at Rahlu and said, "Bro, I've got to go. I do want to say thank you to everyone who took time out of their evening for this. It means a lot to me, and probably more ways than I even realize. Either way, I appreciate your concern, and again, Thank You.

Victor, Crendon, and you too, Zachary; Rahlu, the floor is now yours, and I'll see you later."

Seth walked toward Isabella, who led him towards the kitchen door. As he pushed the door open, he saw Catrina standing there, in her boots and her jacket, waiting for him to walk her home, as they agreed, earlier.

"There you are. I thought I was going to have to come and drag you out of the turkey coop soon. I told you I wasn't going to let you brush me off," Catrina said, smiling.

Seth helped Catrina put her coat on and quietly said to her, "Believe me, Sugar, you've nothing to worry about."

CHAPTER 22

The two quietly escaped out the back door of the restaurant and decided to take a stroll toward the Lighthouse, the opposite direction of Staircase. They walked arm in arm to stay warm, the enjoyment of being together with nothing, nor nobody to bother them. A rare chance to enjoy each other, and Seth wanted to take advantage of it to tell Catrina how much she meant to him, with a tendency to show her the special feelings she brought into his life. Feelings and emotions he was experiencing that he never knew existed until now. Still, Seth was mind-boggled. He wanted to express and show everything he felt for her, but, because of the episode previously, he didn't know how to go about getting answers to three important questions; how to, where and when to attempt it without making Catrina feel pressured in any way. It had to be done appropriately or not at all. He didn't want to ruin the opportunity.

As the two walked their way around the docks, heading back toward Staircase, Catrina said, "I think this is the most fun I've ever had to myself since, well, ever. No kids, no duties, and No Pete and Stanley. That's like a dream come true." The two of them laughed.

At the front door to Staircase, Seth was determined to let Catrina tell him what her plan was going to be for the evening, hoping she would want to spend the free time together with him. He wanted to stay there to visit longer, but also, he didn't want to push it.

"I had a great time, Seth. I look forward to doing this again, real soon. I can't wait for this cold to go away so spring weather can warm this place up."

"This time was perfect for me. I would like this to go on endlessly with the warmer weather; definitely warmer. But even the cold is fine by me, that way I get to hold you more and longer," Seth told her, as he stepped up, gave her a big, tight hug, rubbed her shoulders and gave her a kiss.

"I would like to invite you in, but I know I'll be immediately occupied once I get undressed. We'll try to spend some more time like we did before, in the living room, in front of the fireplace," she told him, with a naughty grin on her face as she looked at him. She leaned toward him and gave him a long, warm kiss, and went into Staircase.

As Seth made his way through the snow, on his way back to the Inn, his pace was of no hurry. Catrina was more precious to him and he was now used to, or even immune to the disturbing feel of extreme cold arctic air.

When he got to the Inn, he walked around to the back door, surprising Pete, who was rotating the firewood in the shed, getting ready to out and bring in more for the evening and the morning.

"Oh, shhhh" Pete expressed, surprisingly.

"Didn't even see you come in. I think my heart skipped a beat."

"I'm sorry, Pete. I was daydreaming when I got to the door. Anyway, do you want some help?" Seth asked.

"Oh, I always like some help. The only problem is Mom said I'm to do it by myself. She said you and Rahlu do too much around here, already."

"Don't worry about it. I'll tell her you told me not to. I just need to do something to keep my mind off of my present problem. Well, I can't consider it a problem, but, I am very confused on how to handle it."

As the two began walking out to the barn to get more wood, Pete was intrigued on exactly what kind of person Seth was. While they loaded armfuls of split wood Pete said, "What's it like back where you and your brother are from. How big is the town? Is it anything like here, in Darquata?"

Seth said, "Dechnadi isn't much different than Darquata. The part that I like is Isabella's. Back home, there's one place like that called "The Bouy."

Pete replied, "The Buoy? What's that?"

"The Buoy is a little 'greasy spoon' place. It has excellent food and drinks, even some soda fountain specialties. The thing that I find is a better quality in Isabella's is that Isabella doesn't run her restaurant as a 'bar and grill', like the Buoy. After the day ends and most of the stores and businesses close, all the action is found at the Buoy. It's really not that bad; a good, home-like place to bring your family to eat, during the day. Just don't bring the kids after dinner hours."

"Why not?" Pete asked.

Seth said, "The Buoy was a bar at night. Too many people considered that place like home. The draft beer, to them, was like a remedy. The remedy to get rid of their hangover is all. If you met some of these sailors from there you'd think they were men like Victor and Crendon, or even Ralph. But run into those guys on their way home after hours, you'd think you met barbarians of a different world. You'd see different faces and they'd all a far different tone of voice. You'll probably hear them slurring as they talk.

The funny thing about that is, some are only talking to themselves."

Pete got a laugh out of that. "You wait until you're here for a little while longer. A regular Saturday night is a bunch of chaos in Darquata, too. Only Isabella will not allow that in her place. She won't even serve those guys if they can't walk through the door by themselves. Her ritual is "If you can't walk straight, you don't belong HERE!'"

"Where do all the crewmen go for their drinking in Darquata?" Seth asked.

"Most of them stay right on their ships. There are a lot of nights, especially weekends, when you can hear those guys hootin' and howling. Sometimes, depending on the time of year, you can listen to the chaos even at the crack of dawn."

"Boy, those crews sound very considerate, here" Seth replied.

The two carried their armfuls of wood to the shed at the back of the Inn. They stacked the chopped wood next to the entrance to the kitchen neatly as Pete emphasized. As they started back out to the barn again, Seth asked Pete, "Do you do any hunting? I mean is there anything you hunt the most around Darquata?"

"Actually," Pete replied, "I was about to ask you the same question. I, myself, love hunting rabbits. Dad and I are running rabbits a lot. What really gives me the urge to go is the rabbit tracks all around the farmyard. Just like that fresh set of tracks right there behind you."

Pete pointed to a main rabbit trail runway that went from the barn, straight to the corn crib, and to many different directions from there. Seth told him, "I noticed a lot of tracks around here when we first came. I've been wishing I had my gun since, well always. I love to be hunting. Goose, deer, ducks, rabbits; you name it, I'm ready to go! I just wish I had my "Bessy."

"Who's Bessy?" Pete asked.

"Bessy is my favorite shotgun. Her and I have hunted many years and have many mounted back home to prove it. But right now, put a gun of any size in my hand, and I'm ready to go. I could really use the action right now," Seth said.

"Truthfully," he added, "My black lab, Conrad, was the real reason. Conrad loved running bunnies. He knew how, too."

"Is Conrad back in Dechnadi?" Pete asked.

"No, unfortunately, Conrad was 12. He's now running all those bunnies in the sky," Seth said. "Have you ever had a dog, here on the farm?"

"No, Mom doesn't really like dogs. I think if she wasn't so much of the 'spic and span' type, Dad and I would have a few hunting dogs for all the different seasons."

In the barn, as the two each loaded up a last armful of wood, Seth told Peter the idea that suddenly came to mind. He said, "Maybe your dad might like to go hunting bunnies. Have you two been out running rabbits lately?"

"We've only been out once so far this winter. Dad's had too much to do, fixing things for all his friends, farmowners around here. I just don't understand why he does it, but that's dad. Hey, maybe WE can go. I'll ask dad if we can use a couple of his shotguns and go out back, jumping brush piles. That'll be fun."

Back in the shed, as they stacked the last armloads of wood, Pete tried to figure a convincing plan to get Ian to allow the two to use his shotguns. When they finished, he went through the house, yelling, "Dad!? Dad, are you here!?"

From the upstairs level he heard, "Yeah, whatcha want, son?"

Pete and Seth both went upstairs and Pete told Ian their idea of getting the guns and permission to go hunting. It didn't seem to take long, until Ian replied, "Is Stanley going with you, too?"

Wow. Pete really never thought about that. Questionably, he replied, "Yeah, sure."

Ian then said, "Seth, I do trust you and all, but, if those two boys are both hunting together, I'd rather you have Rahlu go with you, too. That will put a comfort to me, AND Beth, too."

"That's fine. I'm sure he's all for it. It's been quite awhile since we've been running rabbits. It'll be fun. I'll talk to him this evening and, if he wants to go, we will get back to you tonight. If he doesn't, he'll regret it." Seth replied, with a smile on his face.

Later that afternoon, after Pete, and Stanley finished the chores Beth had planned for her son to complete, the two headed into town to see about Rahlu taking his part in the activity. They both discussed just how they would bring it up to him, and what kind of manipulating it might take.

"What if he won't go?" Peter asked. "Then what will we do?"

"Don't worry, Rahlu loves hunting and rabbits are at the top of his preference list. You have nothing to worry about, I'll guarantee. If he has any reason not to go, I'll just have to blackmail him somehow," Seth said, ending with a bit of sarcasm. Both of them laughed as they came up to the deck at the front door of Isabella's.

As they opened the door and stepped inside,

Seth saw his brother sitting at their usual table, talking with Isabella. Seth thought to himself 'that's an advantage already.' He said, "Hey Bro,' we have a favor to ask you."

When the two got to the table Seth politely sat down next to Rahlu, while Peter sat down next to Isabella, who could sense right away the two had something up their sleeves. She asked, "Is this a good time for me to leave, or will this be entertaining for me?"

As Isabella stared at Peter, with a smirk on her face, he said, "No, don't go. We may need some authority here in a moment," he said jokingly.

Rahlu and Isabella looked at each other with smiles on their faces, wondering what the two were up to. Then Rahlu said, "Alright, shoot. Let's see what kind of trouble you're trying to get me into."

Peter started first, saying, "We were hauling in wood a little while ago and we noticed all the rabbit tracks in the fresh snow around the farm. Seth told me how the two of you did quite a bit of hunting them in Dechnadi and figured maybe we should go."

Rahlu asked, "So what's that got to do with me?"

Seth replied, "Ian said that he's all for it, he's even got enough guns for us to use, but he wants to have you go with us. He says, 'because he wants more adults to overlook the activity, to keep everything under control.' I don't understand why."

Isabella, again trying not to laugh, looked at Rahlu as she rolled her eyes at him; incognito type of look.

"First tell me who all's going."

Seth said, "So far it's Pete and me, but Ian mentioned Stanley, if he wants to go."

"That depends if Mother Adrian will let him go. Who knows if he's in any kind of trouble right now," Peter added again, with a little sarcasm.

"So, when would this all take place; IF I decide I will go?" Rahlu asked.

"Well," Pete replied, "If Stanley is able to go, we planned on tomorrow morning."

Suddenly, from behind Isabella's they heard, "If you guys are going for rabbits, I'M going, too!"

To their surprise, Tara was sitting right there, in the next booth listening to the conversation.

Peter, in his defense, told her, "No you're not. We want to make it back alive."

Isabella knew it was time to convene their argument, "If you keep that up, no one will be going; I'll guarantee it. Now, settle down. There's no reason you all can't go hunting.

"If I can't go, then Max won't go either. Besides, I'm a good shot. I could probably outshoot you and Stanley both," Tara said to Peter.

"You couldn't hit the broad side of a barn," he replied.

"I'll tell you what, I'll make you an offer," Tara said, as she looked at Seth, and pointed at Peter, "You go ahead and put an apple on his head, and I bet I can shoot it off. If not, oh well, I know I can hit a melon anyway." She turned and walked away smiling. She knew that she got under Pete's skin. That was all she needed to do. She knew she was going, or Max was staying home, too. She knew by experience with her father, they needed Max.

"OK, boys, let me get up. I still have things to do to get ready for dinner. I'll send Stanley right out so you can tell him the plan. Oh, I'm sorry, Rahlu never answered your question," Isabella said, smiling at Rahlu as she got up to leave. "Time's running out, I hope you know how bribery works these days."

As Isabella walked into the kitchen, Seth looked Rahlu in the eyes and said, "Well? Do you want to go? It's been since last winter we got to do any bunny jumping. Ian even said he's got the guns we need, as long as you come. He just wants to make sure there are enough older guys, me and you to keep an eye on the kids. What do you say?"

"Well, let me think about it," Rahlu replied, seeing it made them waiting in severe anxiety. A minute or so later, he said, "Alright, let's go get some bunnies."

Together Pete and Seth shouted, "Yes!"

A short time later, Stanley came out of the kitchen and sat down at the table. Peter told him what the plan was and filled in all the details about Ian letting them use his guns and told him that all he needed to do was get Mother's approval. The two of them both knew that with a plan like this, consider it "Mother approved."

"Wait a minute, are you forgetting something?" Rahlu asked. "You do want to take the dog, right?"

Peter and Stanley looked at each other. Then Peter said, "Oh, ok.

But I'd rather take Max instead." Early the next morning, at Staircase, Stanley and Tara had a quick breakfast, got dressed in their wool pants and heavy coats. As they put on their boots, just about ready to head out the door, Tara said, "Max, c'mon. Let's get some bunnies!"

Max came running from the living room, where he was lying in front of the fireplace, and was waiting at the door for Tara and Stanley with his tail wagging, thumping against the wall. He was more than eager to go. He knew what the guns were for and, most of all where to find those 'tasty' critters.

As they were about to walk out the door, Mother Adrian said, "Hold it. Come over here."

The two turned right around and went into the dining room where Mother stood waiting, with her serious look on her face.

"Now, you two, if I find out the two of you cause any commotion; whether it's between the two of you or not listening and doing what you're told, you will not be going hunting again. Not together, or individually; not ever. You better listen to Seth and Rahlu. You know they don't have to take you at all. Be sure the two of you tell Rahlu 'thank you' so he knows you do appreciate his taking time out to treat you to this activity. And one more thing, have fun," Mother said.

Suddenly, Catrina came hurrying down the stairs.

"Hold on there," she told them. Then she came to the front door and gave Tara a hug, whispering, "Be sure you listen to what they tell you."

She turned and gave Stanley a hug, too. When she whispered in his ear, she told him, "Keep an eye on her. We both know her temper." She smiled at the two of them, then at Mother Adrian as she turned around and started heading back upstairs.

For a short time, Tara and Stanley just stood there, looked at each other and then, both looked Mother Adrian in the eye. Mother acted like she had no idea what that was for. She just shrugged her shoulders and said, "Just remember what I told you; Be Careful. Now, you better hurry up before they leave you behind."

"That won't happen," Tara said.

As Mother Adrian closed the big door, both of them jumped off the porch and started running to Traders' Rendezvous, ready to go get some rabbits. Of course, Max was leading the way.

CHAPTER 23

At the Inn, as everyone was getting ready, Ian discussed with Rahlu the different size guns he owned and made the decision of who used which gun.

"Let's see here," Ian said as he opened up his gun cabinet. "Peter, I want you to use the twenty-gauge, the one that you usually use. Stanley, you can use the other one. I'll give the twelve gauges to you two," as he looked each of the brothers in the eye.

As he handed Rahlu the gun designated to him, he instantly snugged it up to his shoulder and stared down the sights. He was satisfied. It was the same size as his own at home and he was ready to try it out.

"Thanks a lot, Ian," Rahlu said, sincerely. "I'm going to love this, even if we don't get any bunnies."

"Oh, if my son can get one, it shouldn't be too hard for you," Ian told him sarcastically as he gave Peter a little punch in the shoulder, to make sure he took it as a joke.

Pete smiled without saying a word. He knew Ian was only joking. Heck, there were a couple incidents when he out shot his father. Ian was smiling at that too. Pete continued to get dressed, determined to get out hunting.

Once everyone was prepared and ready to go, Rahlu looked at Seth and told them, "Why don't you take Pete, and I'll take Stan. Tara, you go with Seth and Pete and stick close to Seth so he can keep an eye on you at all times."

After they had everything settled, Seth and Rahlu, and the rest of the 'clan' —including Tara and Max —went out the door of the shed, heading across the barn yard, through the barbwire fence and made their way across the field to Arnagella's Trail.

After a short walk down Arnagella's Trail, the group came up to a trail that the local trappers used to get around the swampy lowlands, checking their traps.

The kids knew to stick as close to the trail as possible to avoid walking home with boots full of mud. They also knew that the swamp was an easy get-away for the rabbits, if they got the chance.

At the rabbit trail, Rahlu and Stanley walked away farther down Arnagella's, while Seth and Pete and Tara continued heading the opposite direction.

Almost instantly, Max took off, crossing the trail and running with his nose close to the ground. A couple seconds later, he started with his high-pitch howling, on the fresh trail of rabbit tracks. It wasn't long and the howling sounded as if from a distance. Seth took Pete and Tara with him and headed toward Max's barking.

Rahlu and Stanley walked up to the intersection of two trails just a few yards from Max's discovery. They noticed a large brush pile covered with a generous amount of snow. Rahlu motioned to Stanley to stop where he was at and wait for him to get around the backside of the brush pile.

When he was ready, Rahlu told Stanley, "Make sure you keep an eye on that rabbit hole to your left. That seems to be their main runway, so be ready."

"Sure thing," Stanley replied, putting his full attention on the rabbit hole Rahlu referred to.

Rahlu began climbing his way to the top of the pile, cautious of where to step to avoid falling through and injuring himself in the process. When he made his way to the top, he looked to Stanley and nodded. Stanley nodded back anxiously waiting to see the results of Rahlu's brush jumping technique.

Rahlu started bouncing on a high spot on the pile, on and on, until the majority of the snow had fallen from the top into the pile. Suddenly, he yelled, "Stanley, behind you!"

Stanley turned, spotted a rabbit racing through the snow in an attempt to get away from his demolished home.

Stanley pulled up the gun to his shoulder, looked down the sights, and, "Bang," followed by "Bang," again.

That's when the rabbit made a 'stumble' in its race to freedom and Rahlu said, "You hit it Stanley. Let's follow it to see what kinda' damage you made."

The two made their way around the brush and rabbit's runway, noticing an area of dirt on top of the snow where Stan shot the first time.

"That first shot was a little low," Rahlu said, as they continued down the rabbit's escape route.

Up ahead a little further, Stanley said, "I found blood." And as he continued, he found more and more.

When Rahlu caught up to him, with his eye on the blood trail, he told Stanley, "It looks like you hit it good. We'll leave it alone for now and come back with Max when they finish running the one he's on; give him some more exercise. Let's get back on the trail and head toward them. I'm sure there's another brush pile somewhere along the way."

The two of them headed down the trail, discussing the incident, Rahlu suggesting pointers to help better Stanley's future opportunities.

Meanwhile, Pete, Seth and Tara were busy trying to guess the next move of the rabbit Max was pursuing.

"Hey Pete," Seth said, "go over by that big maple tree and keep a look into the thick cut-offs. Sit still and BE READY. When rabbits are being hunted, they nine out of ten times run in circles, coming right back to the area they were jumped at first. Tara, you and I will go over this way to watch for Max. I don't hear him anymore, so the rabbit may have fooled him."

Seth and Tara walked away from Pete, as Peter began heading toward the designated maple tree.

As they walked down Arnagella's Trail, they noticed many deer tracks crossing the trail in many different places.

Seth said, "I hope Max didn't decide to run deer instead. That's a bad thing for dogs. For some breeds it's like an addiction and it's hard to break them from it."

Tara automatically responded with, "Max wouldn't do that! He's been with me since he was a pup and not once has he chased deer. I know my Max, he's not like that!

Seth replied, "I hope not. He was doing great on that bunny. Let's just hope he finds that bunny again."

A short time later, from a distance, Max's howling broke the silence once again.

"Tara, stand still for a minute. That rabbit's very close by now. Like I said, those bunnies always run in circles to get back to their homes," Seth told her. But by the time Tara stopped to stand where she was,

"Bang!" came from Pete's direction. Then they heard, "Yeah!" through the air. Peter added one more for his hunting 'statistics'. He walked toward Seth and Tara to pick up his rabbit.

Before he was half way to it, Max came running out of the thick-its, nose to the ground. When he found Pete's rabbit, the one he was chasing for all that time, by instinct he 'grabbed' the rabbit by the head and started shaking it viciously, determined to get all of the remaining life out of it, completely. Pete walked up to Max and stood there watching, quite impressed and entertained.

"Grab that rabbit from him before he mauls it!" Seth said.

"Wait!" Tara hollered, "I'll get it."

She started walking toward Max saying, "Max, no! Put that rabbit down, now!"

Max dropped the bunny, and started trotting to Tara, showing a proud sense of Tara's satisfaction and praise. Tara knelt down and gave him a big hug, saying, "Good boy." He licked her nose and once she let him go, he was right back to his playground of rabbit trails.

"I'm impressed, Tara," Seth told her. "Max is a well-trained hunting dog. What is his breed, or breeds? He looks like a natural rabbit dog."

Tara replied, "Dad told me when we got him that he's part beagle, but mostly blue-tick. He loves to hunt 'coons, too. Dad would take him out later in the night hunting coons to get their prime hides and then take them to the tanner for some money."

"Boy, Tara," Seth said, "Now, I'm really impressed."

Tara started blushing and headed toward Pete and his rabbit.

Seth said, "Let's go this way. Rahlu and Stanley will be heading this way, so we'll go this direction and leave them some brush piles to hunt. Besides, Max went off this way, so let's follow him."

When the two got to Seth, they turned and began quietly making their way down the trail, hoping to get more action and more bunnies, soon.

At that same time, Rahlu and Stanley came to an area of cut-off tree-tops and logging remains.

"Stanley," Rahlu said, "Go over there by those downed trees crossing one another. Climb up on that tall stump and stand watching all around you, while I walk through to try to kick something up. There's got to be something nestled in there, somewhere."

Stanley agreed and nodded as he started heading toward that particular stump. As he made his way, he kept his eye on the snowy treetops, for any movement in or under them. Once he made it to the suggested stump, Stanley stood tall, on top, scanning over the terrain for any movement in the widespread of fallen trees and treetops. He turned to see where Rahlu was and waved to him to let him know everything was ready at his end.

Rahlu headed toward the back side of the pile, slowly and cautiously in case a rabbit decided to take his chance and run off right in front of him. That's something he considers real competition. He also calls it practice.

"Tara, while we wait for Max to start coming back this way, we'll go over to that brush pile," Seth said, as he pointed at it. "I saw a few holes on the end of the pile."

"Sure," Tara told him, "I need to do something. This is getting boring."

Seth started walking through the snow, around a couple stumps, until he stood across the bush pile Tara intended to jump. A few steps toward the pile and then told he Tara, "OK, go ahead, start jumping."

Tara started to climb up on the bigger sized logs with the more brush compacted in the brush pile.

A split second later, before she attempted to stand up, something caught her attention, something that seemed a little unordinary in a brush pile.

When she looked again, she noticed a very small pink spot, plus a lighter, pink-on-white just inches to the side. Tara focused on the pink she was seeing when she realized what she was staring at. Her heart began racing. She was looking face to face with a snowshoe rabbit, huddled under the brush, camouflaged in the surrounding of white.

She looked at Seth, trying to tell him of her finding without scaring it away.

"There's-ah-ah, rabbit under there," she whispered, as she pointed toward it.

Seth turned his gun around, handing it to Tara butt first as he mumbled, "Be careful and make sure you click the safety when you're ready to shoot."

Tara reached over, grabbed Seth's shotgun and stepped back a couple steps, making sure that snowshoe was still there.

When she saw the bunny, she brought the butt of the gun to her shoulder tight and snug, the way her father taught her. Once everything felt right, she aimed the barrel toward the snowshoe, and when that little pink spot was hidden by the gold bead at the end of the shotgun barrel—POW!

Unexpectedly, Tara lost her balance, from the recoil of the gun, and landed in the snow behind her.

She got up right away and headed to the rabbit to find the varmint kicking endlessly, no pink in sight. She looked at Seth, who was smiling at her, almost laughing at what he just saw.

Tara asked, "What's so funny?"

"Nothing's funny. I'm glad to see you got it. Nice shot!"

"Now go ahead and get it out of there. Try not to get blood all over you. But first," Seth said, "give me the gun. Let me see if there's any snow in the barrel, just in case. Snow in the barrel may crack the barrel next time you shoot it."

Tara clicked the safety to the safe position and looked at the gun. Not seeing any snow, she handed it to Seth and started her way to retrieve her bunny. As she picked it from out of the brush pile, Seth said, "Hurry, I hear Max."

As they started down Arnegella's Trail, they were talking about their incident when suddenly, from out of nowhere they heard, "Bang, Bang-bang."

"That's probably my brother, he can't hit anything, but he loves to hunt rabbits," Seth told Tara, sarcastically.

Tara laughed. Then she noticed movement coming out of the briar bushes onto the Trail. It was Max.

"Max, come'ere boy," she yelled

Max came running to her the minute he got out to the trail.

Seth said, "That last one they shot at must have run a circle around him, or it may have let him run right by."

Minutes later, Peter came walking down the trail toward Seth and Tara. He had that rabbit of his tied to his belt and was keeping a close eye on the small brush piles and treetops as he slowly made his way to them. When he saw the rabbit that Tara shot, he instantly took it for granted that it was Seth who shot it.

"Where'd you get that one from?" he asked Seth.

"I'm proud to say, it wasn't me that shot it, Tara got it before we even jumped the pile it was huddled under. I think you may have something to worry about when it comes to who shoots best." Seth told him, with a big grin on his face and looking at Tara as they enjoyed telling the news to Pete.

Suddenly, Max barked. He noticed, down the trail, Rahlu and Stanley were heading their way. Tara told him, "Hush, boy. It's Stanley and Rahlu. Go see if they have any bunnies."

Max took off toward the two and immediately began jumping up to Rahlu. Tara said, "We know they've got at least one. Come here Boy. Leave them alone."

As the two walked up to the trio, Pete started telling them the news of

Tara's kill-shot. Both Stanley and Rahlu acted surprised, but they both knew it wasn't impossible. While they listened to her story of the hunt, Seth and Rahlu began planning the next step to covering the best of the area.

"We have a wounded rabbit back at the first brush pile we jumped," Rahlu told them, "but there are a couple huge piles we can attack on our way back. There were tracks all around the one, so it's going to take all of us to cover the whole thing. I think, if you don't mind, Tara, we'll take the collar off of Max so he can't get snagged or stuck while he's inside the pile. I'm sure he's going to have fun time. The rest of us will find positions to cover all the way around that pile. Maybe one of us will hang back and watch behind us, just in case."

Once they all agreed to the plan, they started heading back toward the area where they first began earlier, talking about their adventures and the outcomes of their tactics.

As they began getting closer to the specific brush pile Rahlu had picked to flush out, they noticed rabbit runways all around the pile, some even on top of the pile's snow topped cover.

"Seth," Rahlu said, "I see six chutes the rabbits have to get away. Why don't you take Stan around to the other side and keep an eye on the three runways that head straight into the briar bushes."

"Pete, you and I will watch the three trails on this side. Go over by that big hemlock and watch the two chutes in front of you. I'll be right over here," Rahlu said, as he began walking toward the trail, in between the brush pile and the edge of the swamp. Then he turned around and added, "Tara, don't forget to take Max's collar off his neck, so he doesn't get stuck while he's under there. When everyone is at their post, just wave to Tara. Then Tara, let Max have his fun. Are we ready, now? OK then, let's do it!"

Everybody began heading in that direction of their decided postposition. As Tara watched them, she knelt down to get Max's collar and told him, "Sit, boy." Max sat down, right next to Tara. A few seconds later, she looked around. Pete was in place, waving.

She waved to Seth, then Stanley, and then Rahlu; all three were ready to begin.

Rahlu shouted, "OK Let him go!"

"Alright, Max, let's show them what you can do," Tara said. She gave him a hug and then, "Go get 'em, Max."

Max darted to the closest runway chute and instantly disappeared into the brush pile.

Everyone stood in anticipation, hoping that a rabbit would shoot out of the pile, their chance to bag another bunny.

Suddenly, from under the snow covering the brush pile, there came a muffled, "Woof, woof-woof."

A split second later, a cottontail came darting out one of the holes, heading right at Pete. Instantly, he lifted his twenty-gauge, placed the sight on that fast racing rabbit. The bead on the end of the barrel placed on that varmint's head. Then, he led it a little ahead of the head and, "Boom!"

Like that, the rabbit disappeared into the snow. One more for Peter.

Meanwhile, as Max was continuously barking under the pile, Seth hollered to Stanley, "Stan, coming at you."

Just as Seth informed Stan, that rabbit turned direction and went shooting toward the briar bushes. Stan, by instinct, lifted his gun, bead on the rabbit, and as the varmint started darting away from him, raised the bead a bit and, "Bang—bang."

Stan's target tumbled forward into the snow and began hopping around uncontrollably, throwing drops of blood in random directions in the snow.

That one was Stanley's.

"Seth, behind you," Tara hollered, as she watched one sneak out from between him and Stanley.

Seth turned toward Stanley and after letting the critter run to get from in between them, he put his barrel against the tree, laid the sight on the bunny, and "BOOM." That one was Seth's.

Then, surprising enough, a rabbit came darting out of another chute, heading directly towards Tara. Rahlu yelled, "Tara, don't move!"

Tara turned and surprisingly enough, another cottontail hightailed its way passed her, heading straight towards the swamp. As she watched, it hurried its way to 'escape.' "Boom," and then again, "BOOM!"

Tara watched the rabbit tumble and as it tried to scamper its way, injured, into the swamp, Max came out of the brush pile. Once Max got his bearings and his nose to the ground on the rabbit scent, he took off high-speed, barking hot on the rabbit's trail.

Rahlu and Tara both watched Max as he ran that injured rabbit down, got a hold on it behind the ears and took the rest of the life out of it.

Tara said, "Max, bring it here." Max then picked up the dead varmint and trotted to Tara. When he got to her, Max dropped the rabbit and sat down next to it at Tara's feet.

"Tara, did I tell you I really like your dog?" Rahlu asked, in a teasing tone of voice.

After everyone was calmed down and relaxed again, talking about their input and the outcome that it brought, they then, realizing the results, brought to attention the fact that each and every one of them ended up with a bunny from that brush pile. Technically, even Max was to be credited for that last one.

As they all walked their way down Arnegella's Trail, chatting about the details of their bunny income, Rahlu interrupted all by a quick reminder that they were coming up to the location of Stanley's earlier wounded bunny.

"Pete and Seth, you two can head on back to the house. All we really need here is Maximus, and his experienced snout. Tara, you can go back also if you want. Max seems to have his own way of handling himself."

"No, that's OK, I'm staying," Tara told him.

"Alright. When we get up there, you can take Max around the backside of the pile and show him the blood. He should finish the day perfectly. We won't be far behind you, getting back."

Once Rahlu and Stanley got back to the area they left the rabbit, Peter and Seth continued on down the trail to head their way back to the Inn. After they got a good distance away from the group, Tara took Max around the back of the pile. He picked up on the bloody rabbit tracks and his high-pitched howling began once again. It didn't take long, and then, all was silent.

Tara yelled, "Max, c'mere boy. Let's go!"

Seconds later Max came running out from behind the brush pile, rabbit hanging from his jaw. He came trotting tall, knowing he had done his job. Tara got the rabbit from him and rubbed him behind the ears saying, "Good job, Boy. Let's go home."

Max turned and began heading down the trail on his way back to Staircase; a nice quiet nap was next on his agenda. No detours, no sidetracks. Nobody was going to argue over that today. He earned it.

As Pete and Seth walked up to the Inn, the two went right to the wood shed to drop off some rabbits, until the others brought the ones they killed. Pete knew that he was going to be the one responsible for cleaning and butchering their rabbits, so as he made his way up to the back door of the lodge. When he opened the door, the first thing he heard was Ian telling him, "Son, leave that jacket on and go get a couple armloads of firewood before your mother gets back from town, hey? That'll save us both; you know it."

As he turned around and let out a somewhat silent sigh, he started to make his way back to the woodshed.

About half way to the shed, Stanley came up to him and said, "That first one I shot, Max got on the tracks and within two minutes came trotting out of the thickets with the critter hanging from his mouth. He's a great hunting dog. But hey, don't let Tara know I said that. Seth and Rahlu have already got to her head. Be prepared for it."

Pete changed the subject, asking, "How many total did you and Rahlu get?"

Stanley replied, "I got two, Rahlu got one.

After all the shooting I heard coming from over by you guys, I do hope to hear better results."

CHAPTER 24

Later that morning, at Isabella's, she and Beth and Mother Adrian sat at the dining room table, having their morning coffee and discussing, again Catrina's "new" introduction to love and relationships.

"It is great to see her interested in a young man," Mother Adrian said. "Her attitude toward Stanley and Tara seems to be changing. Get this, as I was telling them to be careful, and to make sure they tell Ian and Rahlu thank you, Catrina came to the door and gave them each a hug. He even told Stanley to keep an eye on Tara. I have to say, that's not the Catrina I know."

Beth and Isabella both acted surprised. That was action they never expected from Catrina.

Isabella got up and went to the kitchen for the coffee pot. When she came back, she poured each cup to the rim with coffee and told them of her encounters with Catrina. She told them what Seth and Rahlu told Victor and the other captains. She told them of the experiences they faced on their last voyage from the boat to here when Stanley took them to Dr. Wendell.

"When she heard Seth start the story, she had tables to wait on. But then, he ran into the restroom, trying to keep anyone from hearing him crying. When he came out, Catrina heard more about their experience and then gave them all a refill on coffee. But then she went into the kitchen at a faster pace, I must say. It seemed like something was wrong with her, so a short time later, I followed," Isabella said.

"Wow, that's very unusual. I have never heard Catrina break down like that before," Beth admitted.

"Oh, wait. That's the first part of this. I found her standing at the sink crying. She told me how Seth's story was making her feel sorry for him more and by the time she was done telling me how she felt, she began crying again. What broke my heart was, she came to me and gave me a deep hug. I mentioned to her that we all go through it sometimes and it's what a woman learns from. Afterwards, she 'fixed her composure' and went back out to wait tables again. Since then, she seems to be fine, to me, anyway," Isabella admitted.

"Wow" Beth replied, a little flabbergasted, "that's very unusual to hear; you're talking our Catrina, right?"

"Yes, our one and only," Isabella said. "It does seem a bit unorthodox to me, too. But like I said, she's come to that point in her lifethat's full of options and decisions. Let's just hope Seth discovers how this all affects him as well. I told him that I wouldn't say anything, but, between us, he's quite fond of her; not just talking some little puppy love either. He feels she is the reason they found their way to Darquata. He sounded like it came from the heart, not just from the thoughts rolling around in a young man's head. But that's to stay between US. Got it?"

"My problem is I feel like I'm about to let my oldest child, a young, mature woman, go out into the world and fend for herself," Mother Adrian told them.

Just then the big front door of the restaurant opened wide and with the cold draft that blew in, so did Kyle, Kevin and Kimberly, running straight to the table the ladies occupied. Catrina came in seconds later.

"You three come over here and take those boots off so you don't make the floor slippery. Your shoes are over there, by the coat rack. Go and get those boots off quickly and hang up your coats; then come back here and we'll have something for breakfast," Catrina told them."But first, we'll have to make sure it's alright with Isabella," she added, as she winked at the ladies.

Across town, Ralph and Crendon were feeling a bit mischievous and took a walk to the west end of town to visit with Martha Pepper. As they were about to knock on her front door, they heard, "C'mon in, door open."

The two were astonished by the ornaments, as they entered. Crendon turned around and closed the door. "Take your shoes off by the door, please,"Martha told them."Claire and I just cleaned the whole house."

The two made their way through the beautiful archway, into the dining room, only to be fascinated by all the colors and Christmas decorations and a tall, seven foot, blue-spruce Christmas tree. As both of them walked through the dining room, toward the kitchen, Crendon said, "I'm very impressed. Little Claire really loves that decorating, hey?"

"Sure does," Martha told them. "She knows it doesn't take much talk to get Gramma into it. She went with Stanley and the new guy, Seth, to find that 'perfect tree.'"

"How did they get it here?" Ralph asked.

"Claire said they took one of Ian's sleds and, of course, a saw," Martha replied.

"Where'd they get it from?" Crendon asked.

"Truthfully, I really don't care. It's OUR Christmas tree. That's all I need to know," Martha said. "But I think I'll be picking up those little needles until next summer."

"Well, tell the kids it looks great," Crendon added.

"Yeah," Ralph said. "But that angel on top looks a little 'out of it.' Let me fix it while we're here."

Ralph stepped into Martha's living room to the Christmas tree and reached up and adjusted the ornament's position; turning it, balancing it until the angel set perfectly on the peak of the tree.

"How's that, Martha?" he asked.

"That's lovely. Now the poor thing doesn't look like she's some floozy trying to keep from falling over drunk," she replied. The two, both got a chuckle from her remarks and all three headed to the kitchen to sit down at the kitchen table.

Martha asked them, "Coffee?"

"Sure," Crendon replied.

"How 'bout you, Ralph?" Martha asked.

"You bet! Thanks," Ralph told her.

As Martha went to the cupboard to get coffee cups, she asked, "And, why are you two here this morning? There's got to be a reason."

"Oh, we just felt like causing trouble, and the first person to come to mind was you," Ralph said, sarcastically.

"No, that's not why we're here," Crendon said. "You're going to get beat over the head with her rolling pin if you keep talking like that," he said to Ralph.

"Actually," he continued, "We thought you might want to join us down at the old Brew this evening, for awhile."

Martha, sounding a little disappointed, told them, "Sorry guys, Claire and I have plans this evening. We're going to make some of my old recipes; cookies and breads for the holidays. If we feel a little extra ambitious, we'll make a couple batches of perogies. As I said, it depends on how I feel after the sweets are made. You know there's always the possibility that I NEED that drink after," she added.

As the two sat chatting and drinking their coffee with Martha, the sound of her big front door interrupted them, followed by, "Hello, Gramma?"

Immediately Martha replied, "In here, honey,"

Seconds later, Claire came walking in, surprised to find the two men visiting Grandma. She went straight to Martha, giving her a big, but light hug, followed by a sweet kiss on the cheek.

She then said, "Hello, men. You two must be here to take your punishments for 'something-or-other.' She walked to the cupboard for a coffee cup with a smirk on her face.

"Not exactly, but don't give her any ideas, kid. OK?" Ralph said. "If we're getting' a beating from Martha, we must've earned it, eh, Martha?"

"Oh, a nice beatin' with a willow switch will do these boys," Martha started telling Claire. "They probably need it, anyway, in more ways than one. I'm surprised Isabella doesn't put them over the countertop for a disciplinary maintenance at the Kitchen. Just picture this; two men leaning over the counter, bare-butts and welts across their asses. Beautiful pictures, eh, Claire?"

Claire shook her head, not too surprised to hear her grandma's input. She couldn't keep from laughing, especially when the two 'mature' men started blushing in front of her.

"Well, so much for going to the Brew for a drink tonight. Truthfully, now, I don't even feel like going," Crendon said.

"Oh, don't kid yourself. That place is your water hole, your home. Besides, they need you there; you're their Bouncing Bear," Ralph told him.

"Honey, why don't begin getting all the ingredients ready, everything we need for making our cookies,"Martha told Claire. "Pull out the recipe book for the fruitcakes and breads. Let me get rid of these two out the back door so we can get started. These guys are 'bad influences.'"

"Oh, don't worry, we get the hint," Crendon said. "C'mon Ralph, let's go before she thinks of something for us to do."

"No argument there. I don't feel like putting on an apron right now," Ralph told him.

As the two went to put on their shoes, Martha and Claire overheard the two arguing.

"Just when is the right time for your apron? I'd like to see it," Crendon said to Ralph, sarcastically. Martha or Claire couldn't keep from laughing.

And, like a feather in the wind, the two were gone.

"What were they here for, Grandma?" Claire asked. "Trying to cause more trouble?"

"Not really. They were trying to get me to go down to the Brew this evening," Martha told her.

"Well, why didn't you take them up on the offer? We can wait to finish preparations for Christmas later," Claire said.

"Oh, that's alright, Darling. The smell of pipes and cigars and especially the nasty smell of stale beer doesn't just hold the ole' Christmas Spirit; not for me, anyway. Besides, I've got my own brandy bottle in the pantry," Martha told her. "So, I figure I can get 'blitzed' without worrying about how to get home. Want to join me, Honey?"

"Grandmother?!" Claire replied.

CHAPTER 25

Later that day and all through the night came a heavy attack from the Meskipit; a severe blizzard rolled its way through the region with huge, heavy snowflakes that stuck to everything. In no time at all, temperature was at a frigid climax, with no show of going away anytime soon. But that wasn't anything new in Darquata. A blizzard was quite common. Sometimes blizzards could put Darquata in a complete stand-still.

Fortunately, all the windows and doors of the stores throughout town were decorated with many different seasonal images. Whether it was snowmen, or Santa's big sleigh, or just the good old "Happy New Year," there was a perfect window for it all.

The following morning at Isabella's, all her decorations were up and the whole interior of the store was helping to give patrons the real feeling of Christmas. Even the frost designs on the outside of the windows gave that holiday atmosphere to the restaurant. With snowfall well over six inches, it already put the ships' crew members who claimed the responsibilities of shoveling and plowing the streets to work. Sidewalks and residential walkways were the top priority of the men. They cleaned and de-iced the porches and sidewalks for the elderly people first. That assistance was, by far, the most appreciated of it all.

Stanley, as he walked his way through the snow drifts, knew the day was definitely going to be slow. Still, that wasn't a good enough reason to slow down his pace through the frigid, brutal winds whipping around with the snow-belts, continuously dumping generous amounts of snow. To Stanley, that was reason enough to pick up the pace.

When he got closer to the store windows, he could see movement inside the windows and lights on; something not likely to happen so early in the morning. As he walked inside and shook the excess snow from his hat and jacket, he noticed that Isabella already had the aromas of bacon and toast, and of course, coffee floating through the whole restaurant.

"There he is," Victor said, with a slight sarcastic tone. "We were wondering where you were. Sleeping in, today?"

"I wish," Stanley replied, in a stern tone of voice.

Just then, Isabella came out the door to the kitchen with three break-fast plates in her hands and a full pot of coffee hanging from her apron's string. As she walked toward the 'turkey coop' table, she noticed Stanley and told him, "Good morning, we obviously won't be busy this morning, so take your time. I just made breakfast for these guys so they are all set and ready to move that damn snow; if it ever decides to lighten up."

That was a real relief to Stanley. He could relax and take his time getting everything set and prepped for the day.

As Isabella put the men's orders down on the table in front of them, she said, "Go ahead and have a cup of coffee and wake up a little more. These guys can't talk and eat at the same time, and I enjoy the silence, too."

Stanley laughed as he noticed the place quieted right down, instantly.

As Isabella walked by him, heading back into the kitchen, she quietly whispered to him, "See? I told you. Don't you just love it?"

On the morning before Christmas, Seth and Catrina made their way through the snow, on their way to the Traders' Rendezvous to help Beth finish her fruit pies and prepare the turkey Ian and Peter had butchered the night before. Suddenly, their conversation was interrupted.

"Hey, what's this?" Seth asked, as he picked up a piece of paper lying on the top of the snow. As he opened it up, his eye brows raised high on his forehead.

"What is it?" Catrina asked.

"I really can't tell, but I think it's for you," Seth replied.

Catrina looked Seth right in the eye. She grabbed the paper from him, noticing the smirk on his face.

"Alright, what are you up to?" she asked.

"This is my Christmas present for you. I only acted as if I found it. Truthfully, I've had it in my pocket since Tuesday," Seth told her. "It's nothing expensive, but I do want you to know just how amazing you make me feel when you're with me. I just hope you like it."

It read:

To My Catrina

Catrina, it's the beauty in your smile
You're like the blossoms, on the flowers, out in the wild...
So giving, so tender, and a pure delight
With a sweet, loving fragrance

on a warm summer night…
You've got a voice that's sounds like sweet lullabies
Facial expressions so radiant and bright
Like a beautiful starburst in the moonlight…

Nervously and anxiously waiting for Catrina's feedback regarding his gift for her, time seemed to be at a complete halt to Seth, not knowing what to expect.

Minutes later, Catrina's hands dropped down by her side and her head hung facing the ground. When she looked up at Seth, he noticed her tears running down her face.

"Hey, what's wrong? I'm sorry if it's…"

"No, there's nothing wrong with it. I love it. I just haven't had someone do this for me before. I really don't know what to say," Catrina told him.

She leaned to Seth, to hug him, with Seth holding tightly now. Their hug lasted for a generous amount of time, until Seth told Catrina, "I think we need to get to the Inn, before we freeze. But, we will keep this between US until tomorrow. Then we will let everyone know about us at the same time; on Christmas. Agreed?"

"Agreed," Catrina replied.

The two made their way to the Traders' Rendezvous, throwing snowballs at each other and having some fun along the way. They kept a fast pace to get themselves indoors, out of the present frigid weather.

As they walked into the front door at the Inn, Catrina yelled, "Beth, we're here."

"I'm in the kitchen, Catrina," Beth replied.

When the young couple walked into the kitchen, Beth was a little surprised to see Seth with her. She then added, "Seth, your brother and my son are out in the wood shed."

"You don't think I want to go out there again, do you?" Seth replied.

"Well," Beth said, with a hint of sarcasm, "we could put you to work here, in the kitchen. We've still got potatoes that need peeling, or those dirty pots and pans setting on the counter, if you'd rather."

He looked at Catrina, who stood there smiling, as a tease. And, with a roll of his eyes, he was gone in an instant.

"Well, that wasn't hard," Catrina commented.

"Oh, he's just like any other man. Even if they cook us a nice dinner, the dishes will set until we take care of them. Mark my words, some men do have the knack for cooking, but we can't have 'everything,' believe me, Dear."

The two women laughed and continued to accomplish all they had yet to prepare for their upcoming Christmas Dinner.

Out at the wood shed, as Seth pushed the door open and stepped in, Pete and Rahlu stood there, a bit startled to see him.

"I thought you were at the Staircase for the morning, Bro," Rahlu said. "What made you decide to come out here?"

"I came out with Catrina. She's helping Beth get things ready to take to Staircase later, for the dinner tomorrow. They told me I could come out and help you two, or stay and help with dishes."

"Ooh, good choice!" Pete told him. "I know my mother and if she knows there's a dishwasher in the kitchen, she dirties twice as many dishes, I swear."

Seth started to help stack the split wood and the three began discussing how everything went down during their hunting excursion. It was a look at the whole day from three different points of view. They all had their descriptions of the tactics and many details in their experiences. Until Rahlu hit the one "chapter" that the other two seemed to be dismissing...Tara!

"When did Tara bag her bunny? How did she go after it?" Rahlu asked.

"Tara did as well as the rest of us," Seth said, "and I'll vouch for that, too. She was about to jump a brush pile when she looked at me with a 'goofy' look on her face."

"She's always got that 'goofy' look on her face," Peter replied.

"Well, truthfully, I wouldn't be criticizing her," Rahlu told him, "She did just as well as you, Pete, and she didn't have to shoot as much, either."

Peter quieted right quickly, starting to throw blocks of wood onto the wood pile. His new attitude was really noticeable, too.

"Oh, settle down, Pete. I was only teasing you.

See how easy it is to lose your temperature when someone helps, by aggravating," Rahlu said. "Sometimes it's obvious to see when you're teasing her, and one day, don't be surprised if she 'cold-cocks' you right alongside the head. That will be the day of enlightenment for you. That is, if you keep going on treating Tara like you do. Anyway, tell us the rest of it, Seth."

"She described to me that she was actually staring in the eye of a snowshoe. We both stepped back and I gave the gun to her cautiously.

She peeked over the log to where she spotted it earlier, lifted the barrel and, well, that was all they wrote in that story. Besides, to me, Max did the best of the bunch chasing all five of those out of the one brush pile," Seth said.

"OK. I do agree with you there." Pete said. "Max should get some prize for his performance, don't you think?"

"Well, between the three of us that dog got his prize every time he brought a dead rabbit to Tara; every time, she gave him the loving massage behind the ears.

That back foot began thumping the ground by reflex reacting to the loving he shared with Tara," Rahlu said. "That's a true friendship with a hunting dog, no need for anything else."

The three were just finishing up stacking all the wood that Ian split earlier, when from a distance, they heard their names being called at the house.

"We're coming!" Pete yelled. He then said, to the two brothers, "Well, it was fun…Yeah, right."

Seth and Rahlu looked at each other, both gave a laugh and the three opened the door and started their way back to the Inn.

"Hey, can you two please keep our talk between us, ONLY!? If my mom finds out that I've been mean to Tara, my ass is grass; and my future doesn't look too pretty either," Peter told them, ending with a slight sound of despair.

"Oh, don't worry, kid. You're safe with us," Rahlu told him, with true confidence. "We've both been in those shoes, and if anybody knows when and what not to say to your parents, we do. Right, Bro?"

"That's for sure. We can help you there. Just don't try to use us when you're trying to hide things from your folks. We will try our best to remain quiet, but we won't tell your parents any fibs. From that point on, you're on your own," was Seth's reply.

"Great," Pete said, as the trio came walking to the back door of the kitchen, at the Inn.

With the back draft of the many aromas that were all combined in the kitchen, all three knew there was some reason, other than tasting, that Beth called them in. Pete knew he wasn't going to ask just what that reason was. He learned all about that much sooner.

Rahlu was the most curious, and as he lifted the lid of a big kettle simmering on the back burner of the stove, he asked Beth, "What can we help you with?"

Peter swiveled his head and looked him in the eye, as if he was saying, 'Dude, did you hear yourself?'

Seth stared directly at Catrina. He could see in her eyes that there was something the two women had planned for the men to tackle. Something they wouldn't want to do by themselves, if they didn't have to. Something, he knew, had to do with being out in the cold...again.

"Please, take a seat at the table. Let me get you guys some coffee. Would you like something to nibble on —a muffin or something?" Beth said.

Graciously, Beth poured them a cup of coffee while Catrina brought a tray of freshly baked minced meat muffins, a recipe of Beth and Ian's that was a part of the family for the season. It was a recipe everyone loved in Darquata. A holiday 'goody' that many people asked about. Even Isabella wanted to try the recipe. But that was a no-no, to Beth. It was something she cherished, and she was not going to lose the family values to others' curiosity.

Once everyone had sat down at the kitchen table, Beth began to lead the conversation to the next important task; getting everything they had prepared previously, through the snow, and the cold, all the way to Staircase. Where many, year after year, spent their Christmas Eve, enjoying a celebration to be shared with the many others they loved; the orphanage.

"The next thing we want to ask your help with is this..." Beth said stalling along the way, leaving everyone of them over-anxious for the results.

"We have almost all the foods prepared and just one step from full-completion. That one step is..." again the mind games of stalling, "Getting everything over to the Staircase. I know the snow is going to be a problem already, but I was wondering if you may have some ideas," Beth asked.

Spontaneously, Rahlu, Seth, and even Pete replied, "The sled!"

CHAPTER 26

After that, it didn't take long for the crew to develop a tactic for getting all that was ready to the Staircase to be served, on time. Discussed was the securing of the items to the sled, the route that should be taken and, of course, how long was the estimated time going to be for getting there. But once all was established and decided, the men finished their muffins and coffee and started getting dressed for their upcoming journey. A short time later, the three walked out the door, headed toward the barn to get the horses hooked up to the sleigh; laughing and pushing each other in the snow, like young boys do.

Inside, looking out the window at the kitchen sink, stood Beth and Catrina, watching them act like kids, as they began to accomplish what was decided for them to do.

Beth leaned over toward Catrina whispering, "See? As I said, 'It doesn't take much at all. Just let them think it's their idea and the rest of it rolls all together, as easy as a 'no-bake' cookie."

Catrina turned to look at her, face to face, knowing well enough the outcome was like talking to the infants she watched over. Then she had to say, "I admit, if I would have thought like this sooner, Staircase would even have a whole new paint job, and Stanley would really love me for it, too."

The two women just looked at each other, laughed for a second, and then began putting things together ready for the cold haul through the snow.

At Staircase, Mother Adrian, Stanley and Claira, were getting all preparations complete in the kitchen, while Martha Pepper and Tara were putting table cloths and dinner ware on the dining room table and other serving tables waiting for the people to start showing up for the big Christmas Eve Dinner.

A short time later, the big front door opened and in whipped a frigid breeze. With that cold came Isabella and Victor. As the two were removing their boots and jackets, Isabella hollered, "Mother, we're here!"

Instantly, the little triplets, Kimberly, Kevin and Kyle, came running out from the living room. Like a magnet, Kimberly ran straight to Isabella and grabbed her leg, giving her a tight hug.

Kevin and Kyle headed straight to Victor, who was standing there waiting for them, a little excited, himself. They were two of the many kids in Darquata who called him 'Grampa.'

When the two boys reached him, Vic grabbed both boys. Once they both got their arms around his neck, he picked them up, off the floor. As the two held tightly, Victor gave them a big squeeze, making the two boys start laughing until Vic finally put them down.

"The three of you go play now," Mother said as she walked through the dining room to greet them. "Let Grampa and Grandma in the door. They will be here for awhile. Now, go play."

In single file, the three disappeared into the living room.

"Oh, they don't bother us, you know that. Right, Victor?" Isabella said. "They'll probably be of great help, trying to keep this ole' Fart out of trouble, anyway."

The two ladies both snickered. Victor, sarcastically put his nose high in the air, with a smirk on his face, trying to act as if they irritated him. The two women walked into the dining room leaving Victor deserted and all alone.

Suddenly, he heard, "To me, Vic…"Stanley said, while was coming down the big staircase from upstairs, "That's my cue to get lost, before they find something for us to do."

Not a split second later, from the kitchen they heard, "The boys are here from the Inn. Stanley, go ahead and help them bring in the food they brought from Beth and Ian. Hurry, before it all gets cold!"

Stanley looked at Victor with a serious look telling him, "See what I mean? Quick, run. Get away from here, while you still can!" Then, he walked toward the kitchen with a funny grin on his face.

Victor decided to go into the living room and play with the kids.

"Stanley!" Mother yelled again.

"Hold on, I'm right here," he replied, walking through the kitchen and down the back stairwell to the door. When he opened the door, Rahlu said, "Stanley, come here, quick."

Stanley slipped on a pair of galoshes without any shoes, and ran out the doorway, propping the door open for the convenience.

As he got to the sleigh, Seth called him to grab the turkey.

"Take the bird first," Seth told him, "and make sure it's put right into the oven."

As he picked up the bird, he said, "Damn, Pete, your old man went all out to provide enough bird, hey?"

Peter just smiled as he picked up two pies and followed him to the stairwell.

"Get out of the way!" Stanley yelled, humorously. "I got the bird! Open the oven!"

As he got into the kitchen, Isabella stood waiting for Pete to come to the door.

"I'll take those here, Pete," she said, as she took the pies from him. Peter turned around and went right back out to retrieve some more.

As he made his way back to the sleigh, he passed Seth, hurrying to the door with a box marked, 'Potato Salad/Ambrosia'.

When he stepped in the doorway, Isabella told him, "Take that right over to the fridge. It's not like it's going to go bad or something, hey, Seth?" She said jokingly.

Then, one after another, came Pete again, followed by Rahlu, who said, "This is the stuffing, take it straight to the oven." He handed the big pan to Mother Adrian.

"If we have any room left for it," Mother said, smiling.

As time passed and the daylight was on its way out, everybody was starting to worry what was taking Ian and Beth and Catrina so long? Once the question made its way to Seth, he was also one of those to worry the most. Where was his Catrina?

Discretely, Rahlu pulled his little brother to the empty pantry and told him, "Slow down, Bro! We will give it another half hour and then we will to find them."

"That's too long! How do we know they're not lying deep in some snow drift, for any 'God only knows' reason and freezing stiff as a board?" Seth replied.

"OK, OK!" Rahlu refrained, "Let me get my shoes and coat and then we'll take the sleigh back on the trail to find them. It hasn't been that long, so I truly don't think they're in any kind of real danger. Besides, Ian's there, and I really don't think those two women need much help, anyway, you know that."

Still, the heavy snowfall continued to come down. A short while later, Seth and Rahlu, and even Pete, were preparing the sleigh horses, ready to head out in search of the trio. A couple minutes later, they were riding off into the darkness, as everyone watched them disappear.

Fortunately, it wasn't too far down Arnagella's Trail, when Seth yelled, "Look! Over there! That's them!" As he realized the distance wasn't far at all, he jumped down off of the sleigh and started running toward them.

Rahlu, as he guided that sleigh almost right by his little brother, stopped and said, "Get back up here! We are just about there, and you don't need to panic, Catrina's sitting on the bench while they head this direction. Now get back up here, before I kick your butt!"

Minutes later, the three boys found out that the sleigh was deserted, only putting Seth and now, Pete too, into an anxiety attack, not knowing what could have happened to the others. Pete was now the one who needed the coaching, as Rahlu kept trying to convince him that his folks were fine. "They probably went home for something," Still, even to Rahlu that did seem a little 'far-fetched.'

As the three were trying to detect a reason for this mind-boggling situation, they heard from a distance, "Hey, we're over here. We'll be right there!"

It was the trio, Beth, Catrina and Ian, riding on horseback through the deep fresh-falling snow. Within minutes, they were riding up to their sleigh, where their son was waiting, almost trembling in worry a few moments ago.

"What's taken you three? Everybody back at Staircase is worried sick, wondering where you three are!" Peter said, "Especially me!"

"Oh, keep your drawers on, Son," Ian told him. "One of the harnesses snapped and we had to turn back to get the one we've got now. Boy, you're beginning to sound like your mother."

Once the horses were firmly harnessed to the sleigh, everyone was in a better feeling of excitement and climbed aboard one of the sleighs. Ian, Beth and their son, Peter was all smiles compared to a few minutes prior and Seth and Catrina were all snuggled together, down on the flat-bed of the sleigh, holding each other tightly, keeping warm, while Rahlu sat up on the driver's seat with a big grin on his face, trying not to make it too noticeable, as he followed Ian back to the Staircase.

When they got into the backyard of the orphanage, everybody was looking out the windows with big smiles on their faces as well. Soon everybody was inside, undressed and in front of the fireplace in the living room sharing many mixed conversations between all.

With the snow still falling and no possibility in sight of it coming to an end, the season had proven to be there to stay. As the bright white started to gain a shade of blue, the daylight hours continued to drift away in the winds.

Still, as the white disappeared, the holiday lights began to light up the town. Christmas tree lights shined out many residential homes. At the same time, the street lights and the storefront windows lit up picturesque, as well.

CHAPTER 27

Suddenly the slam of the big front door was heard. In walked Crendon. Out from behind him stepped Zachary and his mother, Nichole. Mother and Isabella took Nichole into the kitchen to let her get herself comfortable and to get her a warm-up cup of coffee. Little Zack took off his boots and hat, and then threw his jacket in the corner, heading immediately toward the beautifully lit Christmas tree.

Crendon informed everyone that some other friends, Norman and Bonnie, and their children Debbie, Jimmy and Maria, were sorry that they couldn't make it.

"Norm said 'unexpected family decided to show up to celebrate the holidays.' He said to tell everyone they will be stopping by tomorrow, for sure," Crendon said.

Shortly thereafter, the younger kids began what seemed to be a fun rampage, running around the house, chasing each other and causing a lot of commotion.

"Hey!! Settle down!" yelled Crendon, with that big, deep voice that all those kids respected. Instantly, those loud, rowdy kids were as quiet as the falling snowflakes outside.

"I'd be very nice, if I were you," Victor said, "Who knows how far Santa has before he gets here. You all know that if you're being naughty, he will go right on by. So, you better settle down now."

As Victor kept the young ones' attentions, Crendon discretely snuck off into the back room, where Mother Adrian, Martha and Isabella were waiting to dress him up as Santa, a role he played for many generations, and a proud Santa at that.

With all the kids' attention aimed toward the soon arrival of Santa, in a discrete way, Catrina grabbed Seth by a shirt sleeve, pulling him behind her, into the closet under the stairs going down to the front of the basement. Totally surprised, Seth was of no denial or prevention of going with her intentions.

When they reached the planned destination Catrina had on mind, she looked out the door, making sure nobody noticed their personal route to their 'hide-away.' When all was clear, she closed the door and turned on the light. She looked at Seth's lost and innocent look on his face, trying hard not to laugh. Just before Seth was going to ask her of her purpose, which wasn't anything against his will, Catrina told him, "Just shut up and kiss me."

She pulled a small piece of mistletoe out of her sweater and held it up above them with a smile on her face. Seth definitely had nothing against that. So, as he stepped toward her to wrap her in his arms, he reached behind her and, with that naughty look on his face, turned out the light.

Back upstairs, as everyone gathered in the living room, Martha gave a notice to Victor, and he said, "I hear something! Kids, did you hear that? I swear there was noise on the roof!"

At that moment, Crendon —or Santa to all —began doing his Ho-Ho-Ho act as he came down the big Staircase from upstairs. Once he made it down the stairs, he walked through the living room door, where all the children sat quiet, without a movement. Then, again, he yelled, "HO-HO-HO!"

At that, every child in that room busted out with excitement and anxiety, nervously waiting to see just what 'Santa' had in his bag for them.

When all the noise magnified, noticeable throughout the whole house, Catrina and Seth agreed that was their clue to go join the rest of the excitement, before their secret was discovered due to absence. Certainly against his own will, he reached once again behind Catrina and turned on the light. Right then and there, they both knew they had something that neither of them wanted to lose; the possibilities of a relationship that they both enjoyed; a love of their own; heart, mind and soul, and they definitely weren't going to lose it.

As they quietly came out from under the stairs, Catrina straightened her sweater and reached to fix Seth's collar on his shirt. Once more, discretely closing the door behind her, the two of them went the long way through the house to get to the commotion going on in the living room. But, as they came through the kitchen and into the far side of the dining room, almost sure their personal adventure was known only to them, they looked Isabella right in the eye, with her big smile on her face; knowing just where the two were at all that time.

Isabella said, "See? I told both of you that you would be together sooner or later. Was I right? Or was I right? You both got the best thing anyone could get for Christmas. Now, get in there before anyone knows you two are missing. Go on, get in there."

As the two lovebirds walked into the room to join everyone else, in single file, Santa was just starting to pull gifts out of his large guinea sack, or as the kids considered it, Santa's bag. The two of them found a place to sit on the couch and began to enjoy the continuing holiday excitement, giving a secret smile to each other over and over throughout the whole activity.

After Santa (or Crendon), finished handing out the gifts for all the children, he quietly vanished out of the picture, unnoticed in all the commotion.

"OK, now it's our turn," Mother Adrian said loudly. Seconds later, Martha, Isabella and Claira came walking into the living room with their arms loaded with beautifully wrapped gifts for everybody in the room. When they put the gifts down, like a little elf, Martha immediately began handing everything to the person it was intended for.

At that same time, Isabella stepped up to Victor and gave him the gift she had for him; a new pipe with a new white sailors' hat. But before he could say anything, she told him, "That thing on your head is starting to stink! Now you can get rid of it...PLEASE!" Then she took the old hat off, kissed him on the head and placed the new one on him.

"Awe c'mon. That was going to be your present," Victor said with sarcasm, as he turned and placed a sweet kiss on her lips.

All at once, the little kids, together hollered, "Yuck!"

Instantaneously, all the older people started laughing. Until, Martha caught everyone's attention again, saying, "Santa left all this at my house. Ask Claira, she was there when I found them out on my back porch."

Ralph hollered, "Martha, when did you ever get a back porch?"

Martha replied, "Just shut up and play nice." Then she threw him a present. When Ralph caught it she told him, "Let me know if it fits. If not, I can fix it."

She went around the room, handing out something to everyone; Dan, Al, Big Jim, Darwin and Little John; telling them all the same thing; "let me know if it fits."

Claira came from the library with a couple presents in her arms, as well. She walked straight to Pete and Stanley, sitting on the floor, in front of the fireplace and said, "These are for you. I hope you like them."

Pete and Stan opened their gifts from Claira.Each received a rod and reel, with some miscellaneous hardware needed, for ice fishing. Both of them got up on their feet and, all at the same time, gave her a big, extreme hug and a kiss on the cheek. After the three of them sat down in front of the fireplace, Stanley leaned over to her and, in her ear, whispered, "I've got more for you, Honey; after all this is over." He then looked at her with a guaranteeing look of confidence, and a smile with it.

Isabella stood up and told them, "Stanley, for all the things you have done for me and all the time you put into The Kichen cooking for all these 'rift-rafts', and you, too, Pete; helping him and assisting me with the preparations of all this year's events and festivals, Victor and I are having a gift made for the two of you to share. Go ahead Vic, tell them what they have coming."

As Victor stepped up and put his arm around Isabella, he told them. "Boys, after you and Rahlu. Rahlu came home from your fishing adventure with Rahlu out on the ice, we made an order for a shanty to be built for you, just as soon as the holiday's over and the guys at the lumberyard are back to work. Of course, all the extravagant details will have to be added by the two of you. But, since we saw that big fish you guys caught, we figured if we give you two your own shanty, we could have more fish dinners."

Isabella slapped him on his shoulder and said, "Shut up and sit down, you ole coot! Don't listen to him. That is not why we got it for you at all. I swear it's beginning to sound like old age is catching up to that man. We had it ordered to be put down on the shoreline when it's ready. We just want you two to enjoy it."

From the far side of the room, Tara added, "So they know where to look for you two."

Beth elbowed Ian to indicate that it was his turn to talk. And when he stood up to start his little speech, she also whispered something to Peter, making him get up and walk out the doorway to the living room.

Ian began, "First, Rahlu and Seth; we really appreciate all the time you two donated for the upkeep of the Traders' Rendezvous."

"With all the time, help; and at some points, babysitting that kid of ours," he said jokingly, "we certainly wouldn't be caught up as far as we are today, keeping the Inn up and running. Seth, this is for you." Ian then whistled loudly, and Peter came walking into the room carrying a brand new 12 gauge shot gun.

Peter walked straight to Seth and put it in his hands.

Seth was baffled, not knowing what to say. Finally, he said, "Wow, I really didn't expect anything, especially something like this. You don't know how much this really means to me. I never even…"

"Oh, just tell them thank you and sit down," Rahlu told him sarcastically, "Besides, we're going to work it out of you, anyway."

Beth said to Rahlu, "We overheard you, a couple of times, telling your brother how boredom was starting to take over. So, we discussed it with Marcus and reserved you a position next season on the Leveda. We didn't know what to get you, but, we could certainly see that your home was aboard a ship out on the water. PLUS, you both will always have a room reserved at the Inn, without any chores. Did you hear me, Peter?"

Everybody gave a laugh to that, and Martha walked over to Rahlu and started taking measurements around him, startling him, and said, "I'm so sorry, son. There didn't seem to be a package left on that 'back porch' for you. I'll have to…"

Ralph was just about to make a comment, when Martha told him, "Don't you even think about it," lifting her head and looking him straight in the eye.

"You say one more smart-ass remark and I'll come over there and bust you one, right in the lip," she said fiercely, smiling.

CHAPTER 28

Mother stood up and started telling everyone, "We all know there is one person who hasn't even been mentioned yet. Now, Beth, Isabella, Martha and I all want to show our gratitude, thankfulness and, above all, our love that we all owe deeply to our 'Loving Trooper', Catrina. Catrina, will you step up here for me, please?"

As Catrina came stepping through everyone and everything, she was feeling totally bewildered over the way Mother Adrian put all attention on her. Once she was standing next to Mother, Mother Adrian gave her a true hug of appreciation, and began; "Catrina, my Sweet. You have been here for…Lord only knows how long, but since you've come into Staircase and into the lives of everyone of Darquata, we have all watched you grow from a small, sweet and smart young girl, to the beautiful, kind-hearted, motherly type angel you are today. You have not only done so much for every one of us, but you, and you alone, provided the Staircase the warm, well appreciated 'mothers' helper, always being a true relief for many mothers and fathers as well, in, oh, so many ways, so many times. Isabella told me many times how you; and you as well, Stanley; gave so much assurance helping her run the Kitchen at times she needed your assistance, and how you make the running of the Kitchen a more smooth and easy task to accomplish. Again, you are very, very appreciated by every one of us, in so many ways. Now, I do believe Father has a word or two to add…Father?"

As Mother Adrian finished all she needed to say, she walked out of the limelight and sat down at the rocking chair she was seated in prior to her speech.

Father Gideon got up from the sofa he was sitting on and stepped up in front of everyone. When he proudly made his way to Catrina, he, too, gave her a long, tight and well-deserved hug followed by a kiss on her forehead. Then he began to speak.

"Catrina, my dear, you have done so much here, at Staircase, not one of us could recall everything you've done; here and around our town of Darquata. For instance, if everyone will look around this room, right now, you will see that all the younger children are seated either around you or on your lap. I must say, even though there's a huge difference in size and sound, when comparing you to Crenden, the children seem to always listen to you with more cooperation and a preferred determination.

Nothing personal, now, Crendon," Father said, jokingly.

"None taken, Father; I agree with you. Truthfully, it's making me jealous," Crendon replied, looking at Catrina and throwing her a kiss.

Trying to avoid any notice, Catrina was beginning to show tears running down her face, until once again Father Gideon gave her a true, loving hug. Then he wiped the tears from her face. When all was reassured, Father Gideon took Catrina's hand and began speaking once again.

"Catrina," Father said, "If I was to go around the room asking the people's opinions of you all and everything you do, and have done throughout Darquata, I can confidently say, there would not be a bad word said about you. You, my dear, are a true blessing to all of us and we would like to take this time to show you how much we appreciate your being in our midst. We all wanted to give you a true gift for the holiday. Something only you can keep. Not something to give to others, as we all know you would do, if necessary. So, my dear, it is my; or should I say, our; our great pleasure to give to you this honorary key to the town of Darquata. A key to represent the love and respect to you, from all of us..."

Catrina then, unexpectedly began crying, again, and ran quickly out of the living room nearly stepping on Zachary as she raced through the doorway. She ran up the staircase, heading straight to her bedroom. Unintentionally, she slammed the door, almost knocking the pictures down from the wall, vibrating what seemed like every wall of the house.

Catrina dove onto her bed, buried her head into her pillow and began crying louder, muffled by the pillow.

Down in the living room, everyone was baffled. They couldn't understand what just happened. Even Mother Adrian was a bit bewildered. Never before had she experienced reactions like that from Catrina. She looked to Father Gideon, who also, was a little confused toward how he presented the gift to her.

"Don't worry, Father," Isabella said. "Let me go up and have a word with her. We've had a somewhat relative episode before. I think she would be glad to let me know just how and why she did what she did.

We all know it's not like her and I know she will tell me what it is that's bothering her."

Without any objection, Isabella headed for the stairway. But, before she began her way up, Martha came up behind her and said, "Bella, I'm going with you."

Isabella turned around on the first step and said, "Martha, I know you have more than enough experiences when it comes to handling incidents like this, but Catrina has come to me with personal problems not long ago and I think she will open up to me before she would the two of us. Please Martha, let me handle this situation the way I know how. If it doesn't work, I'll call you; I promise."

Martha had no fussing toward Isabella's plan. She had incidents of her own in her past, raising her own grandchildren, and she knew the least amount of people involved when settling the situation, the easier the whole task would be; for both sides of the table.

As Isabella reached the top of the big staircase, she heard the crying coming from the other side of Catrina's bedroom. When she got to the door, she slowly, discretely opened it and quietly stepped into the room, closing the door behind her. She let Catrina cry as walked over to the bed. Then, once Catrina sounded a little more settled down, laying motionless on the bed, facing the wall, Isabella whispered, "Catrina, it's just me, Isabella."

At that, Catrina jumped to sit up and almost slid over, off the side of the bed, replying, "Damn it, why do you keep doing this to me?"

Isabella told her, "Darling, please explain to me what in God's name makes you react this way? I mean, everyone downstairs wants you to know how much they appreciate everything you do; in every way; with love and sincerity as well. I'm sure it's kind of hard to chew, but at least give them the sense of acceptance and let them know that their 'unorthodox' gift is fine in your eye, and in your heart.

"Believe me, if you only knew how long it took for everybody to decide what to give you for Christmas, you'd understand how your unexpected reactions made many of your friends and some of your elders feel about the whole thing. I just hope you can understand how this makes some of them feel. Do you hear what I'm saying? Tell me why the two of us are here at this moment, and not downstairs enjoying the Spirit of Christmas with everyone else?"

Catrina gave Isabella a great hug and began crying while trying to apologize to her about the whole deal. Isabella hugged her dearly, for a short time, but then interrupted her, saying, "There; that's what I like to hear. The hard part now is you going back downstairs and apologizing to everyone, telling them that you didn't react like this intentionally and then letting everyone comprehend that you DO like the gift they have for you. Do you think we can do that, now?"

Isabella looked at Catrina with a big smile on her face and, in just seconds, Catrina's reply was a big smile as well. She, once again, gave Isabella a huge hug and just as the two of them stood up to leave the bedroom to make their way downstairs, a subtle knock sounded on the door. Isabella opened the door only to find Seth standing there.

"C'mon in Seth, I was just on my way out. You two, be aware that everybody's waiting downstairs, so don't be too much longer, OK? Alrighty then; I'll see you two down there," Isabella said, as she stepped out into the hall, closing the bedroom door behind her.

"Are you alright?" Seth asked, sounding helpless and worried.

"I'm fine. I really didn't know how to take their gift. I would rather it be an apron or something," Catrina replied with a smile. "They just seemed to act like they owed me the world."

"Honey, I said it to you before 'you do too much for everybody else, giving no time for yourself.' Everyone has noticed your efforts; the time, and all your love and caring; they just want to give you something extra special...something that you will feel grateful to accept," Seth said.

Seth stepped over and reached out to pull Catrina in for a hug. Once the two were together, Catrina told him, "I know what you're telling me. I just let my emotions take the best of me. I just hope that they all can still accept my apologies, after the troubles I brought onto everyone. I feel like an idiot!"

Seth pulled away instantly. "First, quit thinking like that. Everybody makes a mistake somewhere in life...I just wish I'd made as few as you. Honey, for the last time, you're far too hard on yourself. Just go downstairs and let them see that what they, together, decided to give you, is dearly accepted in your heart. And tell them that you do realize how your emotions took over. Once they see your smiling face, they'll all be smiling, as well."

He leaned over and placed a sincere kiss on her cheek. Catrina smiled and then gave him another, then said, "Alright, I suppose the sooner I get this over with, the easier it's going to be."

Then Seth reached over to open the door. As Catrina straightened her clothes, looked into the mirror to comb her hair, Seth said, "Baby, c'mon now; your gorgeous as it is."

As the two stepped out of the room, Catrina slapped him on the shoulder, trying to make it hurt. She told him, "You're beginning to sound like Victor. I just hope you're nothing alike."

The two chuckled as they started down the stairs to face the crowd.

Halfway down, they heard, "SHH, here they come, now." Walking into the living room, Catrina immediately felt the eyes of every person in there staring at her and tried very hard to ignore the emotions she could feel, beginning to react. But, once she stepped up in front of everyone, she glanced across the room noticing Isabella and Mother Adrian, standing side by side, both with a smile on her face. A second later, Isabella nodded, as if to say, 'You can do it.' She cleared her throat and said, "First, let me tell you all how humiliated I am in regards to my actions earlier. I feel I owe every one of you an individual apology. I hope I didn't hurt any of you in any way. It's just that, well, I'm not very good at accepting things. I know there are a few of you in that keep telling me over and over to take things, just because I did something to help. That's just not my way of doing things. I vaguely remember when I was younger, my mother telling me how life is always brighter when you can do things for others. I guess I picked up on that one early," she said with a chuckle.

"I really don't know why I do things the way I do, but I can only say that I do what I do the best I know how. For me, the best is to help in a way that's, in the end, beneficial to others. Being here at Staircase is the best benefit I have ever received, in more ways than one, but truly, all of you mean more to me than you will ever know. Even you, Stanley," she said, jokingly.

Stanley just smiled, never saying a word. He knew not to make any smart-ass replies, not at this moment, anyway. He figured she was on a roll and didn't want to kill her tone of thought. Besides, he could always make up for it somewhere in the future.

Catrina continued, "Every one of these children all put themselves in my heart, in one way or another. Some, in more ways than they, or you will ever know. I just hope the incident earlier didn't put a foggy image of me in their minds; they all mean the world to me." She looks at the bunch of them, saying, "If it wasn't for you 'Angels,' I'm not sure how I'd make it through the days."

Isabella and Mother Adrian then noticed that Catrina wasn't far from breaking down, again. That's when Mother stepped up and took over, saying,

"Don't you worry, Honey, Not one of these children could ever forget you. I can vouch for all of us, especially the children, when I say, 'You mean the world to all of us, too. We are so privileged and gratified to have you here, in our lives.' And dear, before anything else is said or done on this glorious Christmas Eve, I want you to go upstairs and help Isabella. The rest of us are going to go to get the dining room ready."

CHAPTER 29

Not quite sure what Mother meant by that, Catrina followed Isabella up the staircase. As they made their way up to the top of the stairs, Isabella told Catrina, "Please, do me a favor? Nobody but you, Mother and I know what is to take place shortly. Just tell me I have your FULL cooperation. OK?

Still a bit puzzled about what was going on, Catrina said, "Sure, you know I will."

The two sat chatting about what took place earlier that day; her and Seth's walk to the Inn (without mentioning the secret of theirs), and the time she spent helping Beth getting ready to bring things to Staircase for the Christmas Dinner. After awhile, Catrina came up with the question, "What, exactly are we doing up here? I thought I was to help you with something."

Just then, they heard, "Bella, can you come down here, please?"

Isabella took Catrina by the hand, saying, "Now, you will do me that favor, right?"

More puzzled than before, Catrina still replied, "Yes. Why?"

"Just come, you'll see."

As the two came down the stairs, Martha was coming from the kitchen with a tray of cookies in her hands. At a fast pace she said "There you are. Hurry up."

When Isabella walked into the living room, Catrina followed her, only to find everybody was waiting, impatiently for her. She also acknowledged that the furniture had been rearranged, with the rocking chair she was sitting in earlier right in front of the Christmas tree.

Instantly, Father Gideon started speaking to her, "Catrina, I would like to apologize for the way I presented our so-called gift to you, earlier. So, after thinking about it, and listening to you apologize to us for your reactions, we all decided to do something much more acceptable to you. So, Honey come and sit down right here," as he led her to sit in the rocking chair. He then said, "We know you will like this."

That's when Victor hollored, "Mother, we're ready!"

To her surprise, all the children came running into the living room to seat themselves at the foot of the rocker. Kimberly climbed up onto her lap as Kevin and Kyle climbed on the arms of the chair to sit with their heads on her shoulders. Tara sat down in front of the chair and Stanley and Peter stood behind all of them.

Bewildered, and somewhat confused, Catrina was about to ask, "What's going on?" when Mother came walking into the room, with on old-time camera in her hand.

Before anything else could be said, Martha came over to the chair and put that tray of cookies on Catrina's lap, telling Kimberly, "Now, you hold on to these real tight, like we said, OK?"

Kimberly nodded and grabbed the tray, sitting motionless until everyone heard Mother yell, "OK, everybody 'say cheese."

That's when everyone in the room screamed, "CHEESE!"

Suddenly, everyone in the room was blinded by the flash of the camera. By the time Catrina could see anything, Mother, Isabella, Beth and Martha were standing around her and the tree. Then Victor said, "Ready? Smile, now!"

Once again, "FLASH!"

Catrina was now totally blinded by the picture taking. Then Isabella said, "Alright, darling, we're done now. I hope it didn't scare you."

Martha Pepper then said, "I think I pee'd my pants," sarcastically. The whole room was in laughter.

Mother then started to tell Catrina what their intentions were and why they made it a big surprise.

"My Dear, as Father said earlier, we apologize for putting you through the emotional trauma you experienced because of our inconsideration and taking it for granted that you would truly accept the idea of a gift we thought to give you for Christmas. After that previous incident, and knowing how shy you can be, we did have this planned for a few weeks. Catrina, I want you to understand, you mean so much to me. All the things you have done and assisted me with and watching your love for the children, I'm not sure what I'm going to do when you leave Staircase."

"Mother, why are you thinking like this? The reason I was acting the way I did, is because everybody was being so nice. As I said earlier, I do what I do because I want to. Besides, whoever told you that I am going to leave Staircase, truthfully, doesn't know what they're talking about. There isn't, and never will be any plan of me leaving here. This is my home! If I didn't have all of these children and everybody from town, I can't say what I would do," Catrina said. "You are the only family that

I can call my own, and you especially, Mother, are my 'true' mother. Between you and me, my family is complete here. Stanley is the closest I've ever come to having an actual brother. Tara is like a little sister. Isabella, well, let's just say, is my great Aunt or Mother #2. Of course, Victor is 'Grandpa' and all the men around here are like Uncles, and cousins, too. Grandma is Martha and Claira is a cousin, also. As far as Kimberly, Kyle and Kevin, they're just mine. Everyone means so much to me I couldn't comprehend what my purpose would consist of. Without Staircase and the town of Darquata, I would be lost."

She ended saying, "Mother, I hope I'm making some sense to you. But, most of all, I want you to relax, because your 'lil Catrina isn't going anywhere for a long, long time."

Mother then told her, "Catrina, I want you to understand what the picture taking is about. Isabella, Beth, Martha, myself and Claira, too, decided to plan to put both of the pictures on the wall, somewhere in Staircase, for everyone in the future to acknowledge the people who helped make Staircase what it is today.

After their conversation, Mother gave Catrina a long, tight hug and both ended with tears in their eyes. Catrina looked at Mother Adrian and noticed that she was shedding tears and confirmed her previous statement, "Mother, I'm here to stay," smiling as she wiped the tears from her eyes, again.

At that, Mother suggested, "Honey, by the sounds of things," referring to the noise that was coming from the dining room, "I believe the women may need some help getting everything ready for dinner."

Catrina agreed, putting her arm around Mother Adrian and the two of them headed into the kitchen to help.

After a short time of presenting the food onto the table, while all the men and children each found the chair that was designated to them, the ladies all came into the dining room and sat at the place they knew they were to sit. Of course, Victor, the oldest man of all of them, was seated at the end of the big table with Isabella seated just to his right. At the other end sat Father Gideon and Mother Adrian to his right.

When all were sat and their attentions were all ready to begin eating, Mother Adrian asked, "Father would you like to say a blessing before we begin?"

Father Gideon stood up at the end of the table as everyone in the room sat there silenced. He complimented the efforts put into preparing the dinner table before anything else was said. He told everyone, "Let us all give a special thanks to the ladies who put the incredible look of beauty displayed upon this table, and the preparation made by all the time and effort they put into this luxurious meal. We all appreciate your work toward this Christmas dinner. Men, let us give them a hand."

The men around the table all stood up and loudly applauded to the women and the appeal of their prepared table.

Father then continued, saying, "For all of this, Let us pray; Heavenly Father, We are gathered together here before You in praise of Your Son, our Lord, Jesus Christ, who was born of the Virgin Mary in the blessed town of Bethlehem. He, Himself is our Lord and Savior, and will come again in glory, through the power of the Holy Spirit to deliver us from all evil.

Father, we pray for you to watch over these shipmates and their captains, through the upcoming seasons of dangerous weather and any dreadful accidents that may occur while they work hard out on their ships to bring us the supplemental nutrition needed to survive this next chapter of life.

Also Father, Thank You for bringing us these new, loved souls; Seth and Rahlu, and all the blessing they've brought to us. And Lord, Please bless this food with Your goodness and accept our thanks, around this table and throughout the following year to come. We ask You this through Your Son, Jesus Christ, by the Power of the Holy Spirit, who live and reign with You, One God, forever and ever, Amen."

At that moment everyone around the dinner table, as well as the children sitting around the smaller table, followed, by saying, "Amen." And that is what started the biggest conversation colossal in Darquata; until next Christmas, of course.

ACKNOWLEDGMENTS

Thank you to everyone who donated their generous time and assistance to help complete my 1st novel. I very much appreciate it.

A special thank you to Heather Shaw and Mission Point Press; without you, my books would have never been possible.

ABOUT THE AUTHOR

David W. Stendel was born and raised in Northwest Lower Michigan. He recently published a memoir, *Just Call Me Spaz: Growing Up and Living with Epilepsy.* It resulted with interviews on both radio and television, also a feature article in "Brain and Life" magazine; a nation-wide publication from the American Academy of Neurology. David is often enjoys spending time relaxed outdoors...camping, hunting and fishing.